W9-BDG-906
PORT TOWNSEND PUBLIC LIBRARY
1220 LAWRENCE STREET
PORT TOWNSEND, WA 98368
(360) 385-3181

NORTHWOOD

NORTHWOOD

BRIAN FALKNER

Illustrated by

DONOVAN BIXLEY

capstone

Northwood is published in the United States by
Capstone Young Readers
A Capstone Imprint
1710 Roe Crest Drive
North Mankato, Minnesota 56003
www.capstoneyoungreaders.com

Published by arrangement with Walker Books Australia Pty. Ltd., Sydney.

Library of Congress Cataloging-in-Publication Data is available on the Library of Congress website.
ISBN: 978-1-62370-083-6 (paper-over-board)
ISBN: 978-1-4342-8666-6 (paperback)
ISBN: 978-1-4342-8667-3 (reinforced hardcover)

Summary: Cecilia Undergarment likes a challenge. So when she discovers a sad and neglected dog, she is determined to rescue him. But her daring dog rescue lands her lost and alone in the dark forest of Northwood. A forest where ferocious black lions roam. A forest where those who enter never return. But then Northwood has never seen the likes of Cecilia Undergarment before...

Image credits: Shutterstock (tree pattern)

Printed in China by Nordica.
1013/CA21301913
092013 007741NORDS14

For my American friends:
Amy, Dan, Evan, and Avery Lynne,
Melanie, Molly, and Laurie.

Congratulations to the following people whose names have all been used as the names of characters in this book:

Summer Busch
Harry Mendoza
Anna-Chanel Dolan
Landon Relfe
Danyon Hardie
David Ovink
Matthew Skelly
Natassia Pearce-Bernie

INTRODUCTION

THIS IS THE strange story of Ms. Cecilia Undergarment and the black lions of Northwood. It is probably not true, but no one really knows for sure.

Your big brother or sister (if you have one), or your smart-aleck cousin from Wotsamathingitown, will be sure to tell you that it's not true at all. Which is really like saying that I am telling you lies, because if it is not true, then it is certainly a big fat farty fib. But all I can say is that not everything is entirely what it seems.

Thousands of years ago, everybody (teachers, scientists, government people, even parents) knew that the world was flat. But that turned out not to be true.

Hundreds of years ago, the same smart-brained people knew that the sun and the other planets revolved around Earth. But that turned out not to be true either.

In fact, Earth revolves around the sun. As far as we know for now.

So all I am saying, dear reader, is that you should feel free to make up your own mind about the strange and probably not true story of Ms. Cecilia Undergarment and the black lions of Northwood.

Now, usually at this stage of a story, the person telling the story has some idea of how it will end. But I can tell you quite honestly that I have no idea at all.

So let us go on this strange adventure together.

1
Cecilia

IT IS A slightly odd name — Undergarment. Some people would go so far as to say it is an extraordinary name, which is quite fitting, because Cecilia's family was one of the most extraordinary families that you will ever meet, even in a story. And they lived in the most extraordinary house, in a small town called Brookfield. Mr. Undergarment, despite what you might think, did not sell ladies' bras or underwear, but instead owned a balloon factory. He had a specially built house that looked like a big bunch of balloons — the kind you sometimes see in cartoons, usually flying into the sky with a small, frightened boy on the end of the string.

The Undergarment house rose six stories high and bulged out in the middle (as a bunch of balloons should) and was made of balloon-like globes of all kinds of colors.

If you saw it from a distance, you would say, *There's a big bunch of balloons tethered to the ground.* And if you saw it up close, you'd say, *There's a big bunch of really huge balloons tethered to the ground.*

The entrance to the house was a giant red balloon. Not a real balloon, because it would have popped as soon as you opened the front door. But it looked just like a real balloon. Each bedroom was a large blue balloon, because Mrs. Undergarment said that blue was a good sleeping color. All the beds had mattresses made of hundreds of tiny balloons, and were as soft as a cloud to sleep on. The living room was green, with balloon sofas and balloon coffee tables. In the kitchen there were balloon-shaped tables and chairs, and even balloon-shaped pots.

Jana, the housekeeper, cooked most of the meals. But whenever they had a dinner party, which was often, Mrs. Undergarment called Longfellow's, the restaurant next door. Longfellow's happily prepared all the meals and floated them over in a basket attached to a bunch of balloons on a long string.

Cecilia spent much of her time in the attic, the highest balloon at the very top of the bunch. It was a clear balloon, transparent like glass, and it made her feel like a princess at the top of a tall tower. She would often lie on the floor and dream of kings and queens in far-off lands, of handsome knights in shining armor, and of elegant balls. Through the clear walls she could see all of Brookfield and beyond: the apple trees in neat rows over at Clemows Orchard; the twin spires of the Church of the Yellow Bird on the island in the middle of Lake Rosedale, where the entire congregation went to church on Sunday mornings by canoe, yacht, or pedal boat; the gray shapes of the elephants and the long necks of the giraffes moving past the fences at Mr. Jingle's Wild West Show and African Safari Park; and the mist-shrouded forest and black-capped mountains of Northwood.

It was said that no one who entered Northwood Forest ever returned, and that no one who had gone in to search for them had ever come out either.

Cecilia tried not to look in that direction. The trees of Northwood often seemed to be human, and sometimes they even seemed to be calling out to her. Although she knew it was just her imagination, it unsettled her to think of that dark, brooding mass just a few miles north of her house, and what would happen if the mist that surrounded the forest lifted, and whatever lurked there was set free.

There's not much more you really need to know about Cecilia Undergarment. She really was a perfectly normal girl. At least, as perfectly normal as anyone who lived in a balloon house near a dark, enchanted forest could be.

And as normal as anyone who could talk to animals.

2
A Cry for Help

THAT'S NOT ENTIRELY true, about Cecilia talking to animals. But it's not entirely untrue.

Anyone can talk to animals, and most people do. They talk to their dogs and cats all the time. Some people talk to their guinea pigs or their parrots. Other people even talk to trees.

The thing that is a little unusual about Cecilia is that the animals talked back.

Not in English or French or any other human language, but in their own animal languages — in *woofs* and *meows* and *clucks* and *chirps*.

Even that is not *too* strange, since many animals talk to their owners. Cats have a certain kind of meow that means, *Where's dinner?*, and dogs have a hundred ways to say, *I'm happy to see you. Where have you been for so long?*, even if you've only gone down to check the mailbox at the end of the driveway.

But what made Cecilia a little special, quite extraordinary, in fact, was how well she could understand what the animals were saying.

A certain kind of bark, combined with a particular expression on a dog's face, plus a certain wag of the tail, and Cecilia knew without a doubt that the dog was saying: *Look at my owner. What a pickle-brain. He takes me to the park and walks me around each day, hoping that some nice young lady is going to stop and comment on how beautiful my coat is, and that will lead to coffee, then dinner, and eventually to the wedding chapel.*

And a slight change in the expression in the dog's eyes and the tone and length of its bark, and it was saying: *But whenever anyone does stop to compliment me, he is always too shy to say anything but "thank you" and just walks on. What a pickle-brain!*

Not only could Cecilia talk to and understand animals, but she had also learned some of the few hidden truths about dogs: they are much smarter than they seem, and they often don't think very much of their owners, but they love them just the same. They tend to regard their owners the way a parent might regard a slightly rebellious child.

It must be a matter of constant surprise to dogs that humans never actually get any smarter and just keep making the same mistakes over and over again. Of course cats figured this out years ago, which is why they treat humans with such contempt.

Cecilia knew all this, but she also knew not to let anyone know that she could understand what animals were saying. In some deep, secret place inside her, she realized that this was special and private.

She knew this the same way that birds know how to fly without anyone ever teaching them and that dogs know how to lift their legs when they go pee.

Usually in a story like this, the hero (that's Cecilia) is an orphan. The hero often lives with her evil stepmother or her wicked aunt and uncle who don't care about her one bit and devote all their attention to their own disgusting son or daughter.

But this was definitely not the case with Cecilia.

It's true that she lived with her father and her stepmother, but her stepmother loved and cared for Cecilia very much, and was only a little bit odd. Cecilia loved her too, and had always called her Mommy. She had never met her birth mother, who had died when Cecilia was born.

So Cecilia lived very happily with her dad, her stepmom,

and their housekeeper, Jana, who loved everybody and still had love to spare.

***

Cecilia's strange adventure began on a Friday afternoon. That was often a sad time for Cecilia because school was over for the week. Cecilia loved school. She loved her friends and she loved to play Duck, Duck, Goose at recess and Four Square at lunchtime.

She liked her teacher, Mr. Treegarden, who rode to school on a rickety old bike that went *clickety-clack*. He always called out "Nice to see you!" as he passed Cecilia skipping along Strawberry Lane, and Cecilia would always call back "To see you, nice!" as Mr. Treegarden bumped his way over the cobblestones to school.

Cecilia especially liked learning new things, and at school they were always learning lots of new things. She knew how to do long division and how to spell rhododendron (which is a particularly hard word to spell) and that Reykjavik is the capital of Iceland and that Earth revolves around the sun. (Which is true, as far as we know.)

But this Friday Cecilia wasn't feeling sad.

She was quite excited because she was invited to a birthday sleepover at her best friend Kymberlee's house on Saturday. She would not make it to that party, but she didn't know that yet.

Cecilia was reading a new book that her father had bought her, all about King Arthur and the beautiful Queen Guinevere, when she heard the noise.

She closed the book for a moment, listening carefully with both her ears.

There it was again. A distinct but distant bark. A distressed bark.

To really understand what dogs were barking about, Cecilia had to see the animal, because the sound of the bark was only part of the language.

Still she knew, from the tone of the bark, that something was terribly wrong.

Cecilia walked over to the transparent wall of the attic and looked out.

Just at that moment, the dog barked again.

She saw it immediately.

It was Mr. Proctor's dog, a beautiful Samoyed — the long-haired, white, Siberian sled dogs that are often mistaken for huskies. It was standing with its front paws up against the window on the top floor of Mr. Proctor's house.

The Samoyed barked again, and this time Cecilia

understood it perfectly. The lowering of the ears, the widening of the eyes, the way its head moved, plus the sound of the bark. She understood it as well as if it had spoken in English.

"Help me!" the Samoyed said.

3
Rocky

You ALREADY KNOW that on one side of Cecilia's house was a restaurant. What you don't know is that on the other side was a little old house, in which lived a little old lady who wore too many hats and her bloomers on the outside of her pants. And behind Cecilia's house was an enormous mansion, three stories high, which was still only half as high as the Undergarment balloon house, but was still pretty big.

In that house lived Mr. Proctor, the grocer. He wasn't really a grocer, although he used to be. Three years before, Mr. Proctor had turned his little corner grocery store into a superstore. It was called ProctorMart and it was one of those everything shops.

Along with fresh produce and groceries, it sold clothes and shoes, medicine and books, pots and pans, computers and TVs and cell phones, and just about everything you would ever want to buy.

When Mr. Proctor was a grocer, he was a ruddy-cheeked, big-bellied, teddy bear of a man, with a brown beard and a huge smile. He was always offering little samples of bread or cheese to the children who came into the shop.

And if ever anyone didn't have enough money to pay for their groceries, he would just laugh and say, "Pay me next week." And sometimes, if he knew they were really poor, he wouldn't worry about it at all.

But when he opened his superstore, he changed. And as the superstore grew larger, Mr. Proctor changed some more.

He shaved off his beard to look more professional. He bought seven different exercise machines, which did a lot of exercise for him, and he lost one hundred pounds. He went from being a jovial, bearded, fat grocer to a thin, greedy businessman in the span of just twelve months.

The smaller stores in Brookfield began to close down. They couldn't compete with ProctorMart's cheap prices. As they closed down, all their customers were forced to shop at ProctorMart, whether they wanted to or not.

And no longer did anyone get anything for free from

Mr. Proctor, even though he could afford it much more than before.

Mr. Proctor had a wife, Adelia, and a daughter, Jasmine. Adelia had been a tall, happy, rather messy woman — big and wobbly, but in just the right places. She was often seen striding down the main street with a huge smile on her face, greeting everyone she met like a long-lost friend.

But when the grocery market changed into a superstore, and the big, bearded grocer changed into a thin, selfish businessman, Adelia's life changed too.

She was no longer seen happily marching down the main street; she seemed to shuffle, and the greetings she received were no longer very pleasant. Some of them were angry and some of them were sad.

Then one day, she and Jasmine left and did not return.

After that, Mr. Proctor began to act in ways that were more than just selfish . . . more than just greedy. He began to torment the people (and animals) around him.

And he lived right behind Cecilia's house.

***

Cecilia pressed her nose right up against the transparent wall of the attic and looked down at the dog. The wall pushed back against her face, squashing her nose, which probably made her look quite funny — like a squashed melon or an alien octopus.

But the only living thing that could see her funny-looking face was the beautiful Samoyed on the top floor of Mr. Proctor's house, and he (or she) clearly had more important things to worry about than whether Cecilia's nose was squashed like a pancake that hadn't been flipped properly.

"What's wrong?" Cecilia shouted down at the dog. It looked up at her quizzically. She pressed her hands around her mouth, right up against the wall, and called out to it again at the top of her voice.

Still the dog could not hear her, so she went out to the balcony.

The balcony encircled the attic and offered the most spectacular views across the countryside — even better than from inside the attic itself. When Cecilia pretended to be a princess, like in her books, it was always here that she would come to stare out at the kingdom and to bestow blessings on her subjects.

It was a little windy, but the balcony had a high safety railing, so she was not concerned.

"What's wrong?" she called down to the dog.

"I'm hungry," the dog called back up. "Starving."

"Are you sure?" Cecilia asked. She didn't want to be rude, but she knew that dogs were prone to exaggeration, especially about food.

"I'm starving to death!" the dog replied. There was something about the look in the animal's eyes that told Cecilia it was indeed true.

"What's your name?" Cecilia asked, while she thought about what the dog had said.

"Rocky," the Samoyed said.

"Are you a boy dog?" Cecilia asked and Rocky woofed a quick yes.

"Well," Cecilia started, careful not to sound rude, "why don't you just ask your owner for some food? He owns a big store, and I know they sell dog food. I am sure he will feed you if you ask."

Rocky gave her a look that would have made Cecilia feel a little silly, if not for the terribly sad look in his eyes.

"I have asked and asked and asked. When Mrs. Proctor was around, she always fed me, because I was her dog. But since she left, no one feeds me. I am only alive now because of the little scraps of food that old Aunt Beatrice drops from the table by accident. And because I lick food off the plates in the dishwasher when they're not looking. Plus I find some in the garbage can."

"Oh my word," said Cecilia. It wasn't the sort of thing she'd usually say, but it sounded quite appropriate for the circumstances. "Oh my word, that's truly horrible! How could someone treat such a beautiful dog that way? How could he treat any dog that way?"

"I have to go now," Rocky said. "I think he has heard me barking up at you, and I'm in for a kicking."

"He *kicks* you?" Cecilia said, her jaw gaping open. But the snowy face at the window disappeared and only silence filled the gap between the two houses.

She went back inside and stared down at the house for a long time, her nose still squashed against the wall. She stood there so long that when she finally peeled her face off the wall, it was red and blotchy, and her nose seemed stuck in the squashed-alien octopus look. The desperate expression in Rocky's eyes was fixed in her brain.

There was no doubt that something had to be done. And there was no doubt that Cecilia was the one who had to do it. Just what needed to be done? Well, that was the question that she still didn't have an answer for.

What she needed was a plan.

If there was one thing Cecilia was good at, it was forming plans — but there was another thing that she was very good at too, which was carrying those plans out.

She wrote *PLAN* at the top of a large piece of paper in big block letters. Then she sat down to think. What did she know?

In smaller letters she wrote *Rocky*, then *Mr. Proctor's house.*

How could she rescue Rocky from Mr. Proctor's house? Clearly she was going to need a clever idea. She couldn't just burst through the door, guns blazing, and carry Rocky off. She wasn't big or strong enough for that, and anyway she didn't have any blazing guns, or any kind of guns at all. She would have to use her brain. And she had a very good brain, which more than made up for not having any blazing guns.

She wrote down Mr. Proctor's name, and next to it she listed all the things she knew about him, including the word *scary*. Then she underlined that word, because Mr. Proctor was very scary.

Try as she might, she couldn't think of a plan. But that didn't worry her, because she knew that often your best ideas come to you while you are sleeping. And sure enough, she woke up in the morning with a clear idea of what she had to do, although it wasn't going to be easy.

Cecilia found herself on the horns of a dilemma. That sounds like a really uncomfortable and dangerous place to be, involving a large and probably mythical beast, but actually all it means is that she had two choices and neither of them was very nice.

She could go to Mr. Proctor and challenge him directly about the dog, but she suspected that he would deny everything. She knew that not all people, particularly adults, were as truthful as she was. And what if he asked her how she knew? She couldn't say Rocky had told her.

Or she could try to sneak into Mr. Proctor's house when he wasn't there and rescue Rocky right out from under his nose. That plan seemed to involve a lot of risks, and sounded very difficult.

First, she thought, she should try the direct approach. Only if that failed would she resort to a desperate rescue mission.

Cecilia waited until nine o'clock, which was plenty of time for Mr. Proctor to get up and have a bowl of cereal and a cup of coffee, but not so late that he would be rushing out to be somewhere.

To get to his house, which was on the street behind hers, she had to walk all the way down to the Peabodys' house at number sixteen. Past the house of the little old lady with too many hats. Past the Smiths' and the Joneses', who were cousins and lived next door to each other. Past

Mr. Stinkbottle's house, with the enormous dog that barked furiously at everyone who passed (but just said a polite "good morning" to Cecilia).

When she reached number sixteen, she turned down the leafy lane that joined her street with Mr. Proctor's street.

Next door to Mr. Proctor's place, there had once been another rather nice house — an elegant old mansion that had belonged to Cecilia's grandparents (when they were still alive). It had been quite dignified and grand in an old-fashioned way. But it was gone now.

A large yellow bulldozer stood on the remains of the house's foundations. Mr. Proctor had bought the house a few months ago and knocked it down so that he could put in a tennis court.

Cecilia looked at the large yellow bulldozer and was sad for the old house that wasn't there anymore.

She felt nervous and alone when she walked up to Mr. Proctor's doorstep. Mr. Proctor was scary enough when she saw him at ProctorMart, where he was trying to be courteous and professional.

To actually walk right up to his house . . . that was like jumping into the deep end of a swimming pool full of sharks.

Nevertheless, she reached out a small, slightly quivering hand toward the doorbell.

It rang — a huge, echoing ding-donging inside the cavernous mansion. Almost any other little girl would have run away at that point, because it sounded as if the house would be full of vampires, ghosts, or monsters, like in an old black-and-white horror movie.

But Cecilia waited.

She readied herself with her best, most charming smile. There was a *thwock* sound from the door as the lock clicked, and then a creak as the door opened a little.

An eye peered out from the gloom inside the house, and then the door opened wider when Mr. Proctor saw who it was.

He smiled a lurking, dangerous sort of smile.

"Hello," he said. "What do you want?"

Cecilia looked at him for a moment as she drew in a breath to answer.

You could tell that he had once been bigger than he was now. It seemed as though when he lost all that weight, he shrank inside his own skin. Now he looked like a thin man wearing a skin suit that was too big for him. Loose folds of skin hung from his jaw and his neck. Dark bags sagged under his eyes, which were now narrow and pointed.

She gulped, and then remembered her mission. "Hello, Mr. Proctor," she said loudly and clearly. "My name is Cecilia. I live over the fence."

"What do you want?" Mr. Proctor asked again through sharp eel teeth, with no attempt to be polite.

"I saw you have a dog," Cecilia said. Mr. Proctor's narrow eyes immediately narrowed even further. Cecilia added quickly, "It's just that, well, I really love animals, particularly dogs, and I don't have one of my own."

All of that was perfectly true, without a word of a lie. Cecilia went on, a little more confidently. "I really enjoy dogs and I wondered if you might let me take Ro— your dog for a walk sometime," she finished quickly.

Mr. Proctor's eyes were mere slits by now.

"I mean, you wouldn't have to pay me or anything," Cecilia continued. "I'd do it just for fun. It's good for dogs to get exercise and then you wouldn't have to take him for walks every day. What do you think?"

Perfect, she thought. She'd said everything she needed to say and she had been totally honest.

Mr. Proctor stared at her for a moment and she smiled sweetly at him. He stared some more. Cecilia smiled some more.

Then she noticed that his face was gradually changing

color. His rather pale complexion was darkening. He still didn't say anything, but his nostrils widened, he snorted a couple of times like an angry bull, and his face kept changing color.

Pink blotches appeared at his cheeks and spread to his ears and his chin. By the time his nose and forehead had turned pink, his cheeks were red and his ears were a brilliant shade of purple.

Cecilia thought that there must have been some awful pressure building up inside him. She was worried that he might burst or die of a heart attack in front of her eyes.

"Of course —" she began, but he didn't let her finish, which was rude by anyone's standards.

"How dare you?" Mr. Proctor said, spittle flying from his lips, but fortunately missing Cecilia. "Do you know who I am?" His voice started to rise, growing louder and louder with each word. "I am a very important man in this town. I am . . ."

Cecilia was wise enough to know that anyone who had to tell you how important he was was nowhere near as important as he thought he was.

Mr. Proctor spluttered and shouted. Most of his words got sucked back into his mouth — only a few escaped for Cecilia to hear.

Those that did come out were words like "outrageous" and "nosy," along with "busybody" and "like father, like daughter," which made no sense at all to Cecilia.

She was nothing like her father and he was nothing like her. She knew nothing about balloons, and he couldn't talk to animals, and he almost certainly didn't know the capital of Iceland.

"I can see now that it was a bad idea," Cecilia said politely, trying to fit the words in among Mr. Proctor's ranting and raving. "I'll go now. I'm sorry if I upset you."

She turned and left, leaving him still shouting and gesticulating incoherently behind her.

She walked all the way back down to the corner, along the alley, past Mr. Stinkbottle's, past the Joneses' and the Smiths', and past the little old lady with too many hats. She let herself into her house and went up the stairs to the landing, then up two more flights of stairs to her blue-balloon bedroom, and she took off her shoes and lay down on her soft, bouncy bed.

And cried.

4

The Rescue

PHASE TWO OF Cecilia's plan did not involve breaking into Mr. Proctor's house when he was away, because that was illegal, and she could be arrested, and she felt that jail would be a very scary place.

So her plan did not involve dressing up in a ninja suit and climbing up the outside wall of Mr. Proctor's house, although the thought had crossed her mind.

She had gotten her idea for the plan from Longfellow's restaurant and the floating baskets full of food.

Every afternoon, even if it was raining, Rocky was let out into the backyard to do what dogs do in backyards. If the yard hadn't been completely surrounded by a high wooden fence, he would have run away from Mr. Proctor's months ago.

Instead, he was reduced to sniffing around in the grass,

scratching here and there for worms and beetles, like a farmyard chicken.

But the backyard suited phase two perfectly.

The only real problem with Cecilia's plan was that it involved some building. Although she was rather clever and could talk to animals and knew how to spell rhododendron, when it came to practical matters like building stuff, she wasn't very clever at all. But that didn't worry Cecilia, because she knew someone who was.

Jana had been the Undergarments' housekeeper since before Cecilia was born. Whenever her father was away on his overseas sales trips, with her mother tagging along to keep him company, or when her mother was off practicing her high kicks at her karate lessons, or making little paper elephants at her origami classes, Jana had been there for Cecilia.

She was a huge woman in every direction and was filled with so much love for everybody and everything that it spilled over all around her wherever she went. All the people she met felt it, and their hearts filled up a little too.

Jana came from the Bahamas, which Cecilia, when she was younger, had thought were called the Bananas. She could still make Jana laugh by calling her Jana-Banana.

Jana sang songs from her homeland in her sweet-like-honey voice, which danced in Cecilia's ears like seashells underfoot, and called up pictures of blue skies and gentle seas in faraway places that seemed real to her although she had never been there.

Jana was enormously practical. She could make a necklace out of flowers or a sailboat out of an old newspaper. Cecilia was sure she would be able to help with her plan.

But even more importantly, Jana would never question Cecilia. She would never say, *Are you sure you want to do this?* or *Don't be silly!* If Cecilia said she had an imaginary friend, Jana would cook an extra meal. If Cecilia said she wanted to fly to the moon, Jana would go to the library with her and find books on how to build rockets.

"How is this gonna work?" Jana asked, turning the laundry basket upside down and tapping the bottom of it to see how strong it was.

"It's simple, really," Cecilia said. "It's just physics."

She had learned about physics from Kymberlee's older brother, Pike, who was fourteen and had studied it at school. She wasn't entirely sure what physics was, but she knew it involved gravity and weight and what made things go up and down, and start and stop, and all sorts of really interesting things like that.

Cecilia was sitting on a sack that had previously been full of flour. She had rescued the sack from the garbage can in the kitchen, and it was now full of sand from the sandbox in the playroom on the first floor of the balloon house.

It was quite heavy, so she took it up to the attic one stair at a time, lifting it up and resting it on the next step, then the next step, and so on and so on.

Jana would have hoisted it over one shoulder and marched up to the attic, singing all the way, but she had been out doing the weekly shopping at the dreaded ProctorMart.

But she was back now, so Cecilia sat on the sack and showed Jana the drawing of her dog-rescuing invention.

"So Rocky climbs into the basket," Cecilia said, "and we pull on this string." (It was drawn in blue crayon on the plan.) "That releases the sand, and up it floats. Then we just pull it in using this other string." (That string was drawn in orange crayon.)

"Like catching fish," Jana said, cracking her knuckles. "It's a good plan, girl. I think it's gonna work." She studied the plan a little longer. "But I think you only need one string. You can let the sand go and pull the basket in, all with one string."

"That's clever!" Cecilia said.

"But you don't know how much the dog weighs," Jana said.

"I looked it up on the Internet," Cecilia said. "Usually a Samoyed like Rocky would weigh between forty-five and sixty-five pounds. But because Rocky is so thin, I guessed about forty-five."

There were forty-five pounds of sand in the old flour sack. Cecilia had weighed it on the scale one pound at a time before putting it in the sack.

"I think we need more sand," Jana said. "Better a little too much, than a little too little."

"Good thinking," Cecilia said.

***

The great dog rescue took place that afternoon at exactly three o'clock. Cecilia's father was out playing golf and her mother was at a charity fashion show.

Most importantly, Mr. Proctor went out for the afternoon and Rocky had been left out in the backyard.

Cecilia and Jana (well, mostly Jana) carefully attached the sack of sand to the bottom of the laundry basket using some wire that Jana had found in the garage. She threaded the wire in and out of the seams of the basket and through the fabric of the sack.

Then, with the basket still upside down, she cut a long slit along the length of the sack, and sewed it back up using a clever stitch that held the edges together firmly, but would come undone with a sharp tug on the end of the string.

Next they turned the basket upright and attached the balloons to the top.

There were always boxes of balloons in the basement. Leftover samples or new product lines. Trials of new colors or shapes or sizes. And there was also always a small cylinder of helium gas, the floaty gas that makes floaty balloons float.

Jana took the cylinder upstairs, while Cecilia shuffled along behind with a box of balloons.

There were large balloons and small balloons. Rubber balloons and silver balloons. There were balloons shaped like animals and some with funny faces on them like clowns or aliens. There were all kinds of colors.

Cecilia selected the biggest, strongest balloons, filled them with gas, and attached one to each corner of the laundry basket using sturdy nylon cord. The basket stirred a little from its position on the floor of the attic, but did not lift.

So they attached another balloon to each corner, while Cecilia sat inside the basket to weigh it down. When she stepped out, the basket shot up off the ground and hovered in midair while the balloons stuck firmly to the round ceiling of the attic.

Jana took one big balloon from each corner and replaced them with slightly smaller ones, until the basket gently floated down to the floor and stayed there. It quivered a little, as if it wanted to take off but couldn't.

"It's perfect!" Cecilia cried.

"Bam, bam, bam!" Jana grinned and hugged Cecilia, who hugged her right back.

When the clock on the wall struck three, they took the floating basket out of the attic and onto the balcony.

Far below, in the backyard of the Proctor house, the painfully thin shape of Rocky stared up at them.

It was a little cool outside, so Cecilia went and got her jacket, zipping it up against the breeze. When she stepped back out on the balcony, she thought she saw a curtain move inside the Proctor house, but it might have just been the wind creeping its way through some open window.

Taking hold of the string, Cecilia gave the floating

basket a firm push. It obediently drifted away from her, dropping gently as it went. Down, down it went, a little too fast, Cecilia thought, worried that it might just drop into her own backyard and not make it over the fence. Down, down, and away, just nudging over the fence, settling with a sigh into Mr. Proctor's backyard.

"This basket flies like a blue-faced booby bird!" Jana exclaimed, smiling. She held up a hand for a high five. Cecilia high-fived her with the hand that wasn't holding the string.

The basket had landed quite close to the fence, but fortunately was still in sight.

"Come on, Rocky!" Cecilia called.

Rocky was standing beside the basket, one paw on the edge, looking nervously at the flimsy flying contraption.

"You can do it!" Cecilia shouted.

Rocky glanced up, nudged aside the balloons with his nose and, with a quick hop, was in the basket. He stood there, waiting.

"Lie down," Cecilia yelled. "It'll be safer."

Rocky obediently lay down on the floor of the basket, curling up to fit in the tight space.

"That dog!" Jana said, laughing. "It's almost like he understands you."

Cecilia laughed back, but didn't say a thing as she tugged on the string.

Nothing happened.

She tugged a little harder, and again, nothing happened.

She pulled it a third time, and when there was no result, she turned to Jana with a worried look in her eyes.

"You wanna go fishing for dog?" Jana said. "You gotta be much stronger than that."

Jana stretched her hands out in front of her, interlacing her fingers and cracking her knuckles. She took the string from Cecilia's hand and gave it a sharp yank.

Below them, the basket wobbled and Rocky gave a little whimper.

Jana jiggled the line as if she really was catching a fish. "Gotta shake out the sand," she said.

One edge of the basket seemed to rise up a little. As it rose, more sand must have fallen out, because it lifted even higher off the ground.

"Bam, bam, bam!" Jana shouted in Cecilia's ear.

Then, to Cecilia's great joy, the whole basket began to float up, very slowly at first, but she could see the constant trickle of sand falling out from beneath it.

As the sand fell, the basket got lighter, so it rose higher and faster. It climbed over the fence and past the second-story windows of the balloon house, past the third floor, the fourth, and the fifth. As it climbed up toward the attic balcony, Jana began to reel the string in, pulling the basket closer and closer until it was right up alongside them. She reached out with a strong arm and pulled the basket toward her.

Rocky, by now, had overcome his nervousness and was standing up in the basket with his paws on the edge, barking with excitement.

"Sit down, Rocky!" Cecilia called out. "You'll tip the basket over."

Together they pulled the basket, with Rocky inside, over the edge of the balcony.

Cecilia quickly reached up to untie one of the balloons, letting it escape. She released another balloon, and another, until the basket was sitting firmly on the floor of the balcony.

Rocky hopped out of the basket and straight onto Cecilia, knocking her over backward and licking her face like they were long-lost friends.

"That's one happy fella!" Jana exclaimed.

"We did it!" Cecilia shouted, more than a little surprised that her plan had gone so well.

She looked down at Mr. Proctor's yard. There was a

small mound of sand where the basket had landed, and a trail of sand leading up over the fence, but even as she watched, it stirred and began to disperse in the breeze.

"We did it," she said again.

5
SAFE AT LAST

THEY DIDN'T HAVE any dog food in the house, but Jana sorted that out with a bowl full of cut-up leftover steak and vegetables. Cecilia gave Rocky some water in one of her mother's best ceramic bowls, and Rocky ate and drank like a king.

Afterward he wiped his mouth with his paws — very politely, Cecilia thought — and woofed a short but heartfelt thank you.

"You're welcome," Cecilia said, and caught a quick glance from Jana out of the corner of her eye.

Jana went off to carry on with the housework because housework won't do itself, and Cecilia took Rocky up to the attic to play.

He wasn't very playful though. He really just wanted to sleep, which Cecilia understood quite well because she often felt the same way after a big meal. She also knew that Rocky would be weak from months of near starvation.

Just then, the doorbell rang. Even that didn't wake Rocky. Cecilia left him sleeping and bounded down the stairs to see who it was.

The doorbell sounded a second time before she even got down to the third level of the house, so the person must have been in a real hurry. *It must be something very urgent,* Cecilia thought, *or maybe they are just impatient.*

She got to the door as the bell sounded for a third time. *How rude,* she thought, and opened the door.

Standing on the doorstep in a shiny black suit was the loose-skinned, bony frame of Mr. Proctor. The expression on his face was enough to curdle your milk and curl your hair.

"Where's my dog?" he demanded. "I want my dog back."

"Hello, Mr. Proctor," Cecilia began, because her parents had taught her always to be polite when answering the telephone or the front door.

"I know you took him, you interfering little busybody."

Cecilia was shocked. Even though she had already experienced Mr. Proctor's temper once that day, it was quite another thing to be confronted on your own doorstep.

"Where is my dog?" Mr. Proctor repeated, narrowing his eyes again.

"Have you considered the possibility that your dog got so thin and dehydrated that he just crumbled into a pile of sand?" Cecilia asked. She thought it was a fair question to ask and, being a question, was not at all dishonest.

"Don't try to be clever," Mr. Proctor said. "My aunt saw the whole thing. Now, where is my dog?"

"I don't believe he is your dog," Cecilia said firmly. "Rocky really belongs to your wife."

As soon as the words were out of her mouth, she wished she hadn't said them. Partly because she'd said something that she shouldn't have known, but mostly because as soon as she mentioned Mrs. Proctor, she realized it was the wrong thing to say. It was like lighting a match near a box of firecrackers.

"How dare you!" Mr. Proctor shouted. "You cheeky little brat!" Words started to bubble out of his mouth with no real sense or meaning, and his face was again the color of a sun-ripened tomato.

"Get out of the way," he finally managed to say. He reached out and gripped Cecilia's shoulder with long, bony fingers, shoving her to one side.

"Ow!" cried Cecilia, reaching up and trying to pry

his fingers out from where they were digging into her shoulder. She was stunned. Grown-ups should never hurt children!

"Where is he?" snarled the raging monster on her doorstep. Then the expression on his face changed abruptly, and he looked up and past Cecilia.

From behind her, Cecilia heard a cracking of knuckles and a quiet voice.

"You take your hand off that child, else I gonna break your fingers."

Mr. Proctor's hand loosened, then slipped from Cecilia's shoulder.

"Cecilia, child, you go upstairs while I talk to Mr. Proctor."

Cecilia needed no urging. She turned and ran up five flights of stairs to the attic, where she found Rocky wide awake, lips drawn back, growling at the noise from below.

"You stay here," Cecilia said. "We need to stay away from him."

Rocky stopped growling, but he circled the room nervously.

Cecilia's heart was beating fast and she wiped her hands on her clothes again and again.

The front door slammed and Jana's heavy footsteps

sounded up the stairs. She arrived in the attic with a phone in her hand.

"I phoned your daddy," she said, "and your mama. They're coming home now."

She drew Cecilia into her large bosom and wrapped her huge arms around her. Cecilia almost felt that she had been swallowed up by the large woman, and the terror flowed out of her.

"That man — he's got no love in his heart," Jana said. "Something done sucked all the love outta him."

***

For the next ten minutes there was silence. *It's like the eye of a storm,* Cecilia thought, *when all seems calm, but the worst is yet to come.* And she was right in ways that she couldn't possibly have imagined.

Her father arrived home first, his sleek sports car appearing like a splash of red paint at the end of the road, then getting bigger and bigger until it turned into a car with a set of golf clubs sliding around in the backseat.

Next, Cecilia heard the sound of an engine nearby. *A big engine,* Cecilia thought, *like that of a tractor, or a . . .*

Bulldozer!

She rushed across to the other side of the room and

stared down as the big yellow machine on the other side of the fence began to move, turning slowly and inching forward.

It was clear that whoever was driving the machine did not really know how to, because the driver kept going forward and backward as if he wasn't quite sure what he was doing.

Eventually, though, it completed the turn.

To Cecilia's horror, it began to advance, like a lumbering yellow rhinoceros, directly toward the balloon house.

The high wooden fence was the first thing in its way, but that was no more than an irritation to this huge beast.

Inside the vehicle, Cecilia could now see the spindly shape of Mr. Proctor in his neat, black suit.

The bulldozer disappeared from view as it got closer to the house, but she could still hear it: the grinding rumble of the engine and the metallic jangling and sharp squeals from the tracks.

Then she heard her father's car at the front of the house, followed by the thud of Jana's footsteps running down the stairs.

The entire house shuddered.

There was a gasping, tearing sound and the floor beneath her feet dropped suddenly as all the balloon-like globes shifted position and settled into slightly different places.

Cecilia screamed a little scream that stopped halfway out of her mouth as the bulldozer crashed into the house again.

Outside, she could hear her father and Jana shouting at Mr. Proctor, although only bits of words escaped over the roaring of the bulldozer engine.

The entire house shook again, knocking Cecilia to the floor. Suddenly, there was a soft cushion over her, and she realized that Rocky had thrown his body over hers to protect her.

And then the most amazing thing happened.

6
HELIUM

THE ARCHITECT WHO built the Undergarment house, Mr. Landon Relfe, had always been a little worried about the design. It was so tall, he had said, and such a strange shape, that it could easily collapse in an earthquake.

He had been particularly worried about the attic, because it was so high off the ground, so he built in a safety feature. There were special tanks and valves that injected helium gas into the skin of the attic in the (unlikely) event of an earthquake.

The idea was simple. If there was an earthquake, the helium tanks would quickly inflate the attic balloon and give it lift — not a lot, but enough to allow it to float gently down to the ground, instead of falling and crashing from six stories up. It was a great idea.

And it worked! As the house shuddered and wobbled,

the special valves opened. There was a huge hissing from all around Cecilia as the walls of the attic began to inflate with the helium gas. There were two layers in the walls, she suddenly discovered: an inner one and an outer *rubber* one. The outer one began to puff out as all the gas poured into it.

The house sagged some more, and suddenly the attic was free of the rest of the house. The door to the attic, which had been open, automatically slammed shut in order to prevent anyone from falling out. Now all that was left to happen was the attic balloon needed to float gently to the ground, as Mr. Relfe had intended.

However, what Mr. Relfe had not planned for was the weight of the occupants. When he had done his calculations about the amount of gas required to stop the attic from falling, he had anticipated that it would be holding at least two grown-ups . . . not a little girl and a dreadfully thin Samoyed dog.

So instead of floating gently down, the attic started to float gently up.

7
Up, Up, and Away

AFTER SHE GOT over the initial shock and the fear that the attic would suddenly plummet from the sky like a stone, Cecilia found herself actually enjoying the ride. The sky was lovely and blue, and she floated along like a bubble in the breeze, drifting well below the few wisps of cotton-ball clouds.

Looking back at her house, Cecilia saw Jana and her father staring at the sky after her, and she waved to let them know that she was all right.

Even crazy Mr. Proctor had stopped attacking the house and was gaping up at her.

Poor Rocky was running around in circles like a windup toy until Cecilia caught him and stroked his fur to calm him down, after which he lay in the center of the room with his paws over his eyes.

The wind was constantly changing its mind, but it mostly seemed to be coming from the northeast, pushing them southwest toward Lake Rosedale. Cecilia was a little alarmed as they began to drop toward the water.

"The warm air off the land makes the balloon rise," she told Rocky, trying to sound calm. "But the colder air above the water makes us go lower. It's just physics."

It might have been just physics, but the farther they went out across the lake, the lower they got. Cecilia thought they would land in the lake and wondered if the balloon would float.

But they stayed airborne as they floated over the island where the ancient stone Church of the Yellow Bird stood. They were so low now that Cecilia feared the balloon might impale itself on the church's sharp spire. But they drifted past it, and over the even older ruins of the monastery, slowly rising as they crossed the warm land of the island.

They dropped again once they were past the island, and the balloon was almost touching the water when they reached the far sandy shore of the lake.

Cecilia thought about throwing open the door and jumping down to the soft, warm sand, but by the time she had thought this and got to the door, they were already past the sand, and rising higher and higher every second.

Cecilia stared down at the tops of people's houses. She had thought that most houses just had boring metal or tiled roofs, but in fact she found that some roofs were quite interesting.

One large brick house had a vibrant green garden on its roof, complete with a small stream that wound its way through rocks and shrubs and over a small waterfall into a blue pond.

Another house had a big circle painted on its roof, like a helicopter landing pad. In the center was painted in large yellow letters, *UFOs WELCOME HERE*. A middle-aged man and woman, both wearing silver overalls that looked like spacesuits, climbed out onto the roof through a trapdoor and waved up at the balloon with both arms, beckoning to Cecilia and Rocky.

But the attic balloon clearly had no intention of landing on the UFO pad. It drifted right past it, heading toward an old man sitting in an armchair on the roof of his house, playing the violin. He stopped playing and gawked up in amazement as they drifted above him.

Farther and farther they went, over office buildings, factories, and eventually over the wide-open spaces of Mr. Jingle's Wild West Show and African Safari Park.

An elephant trumpeted, raising its trunk into the sky,

as they flew overhead. To the untrained eye, it seemed like a greeting. But Cecilia, although she didn't speak Elephant very well, knew that it was really saying, "What the heck is that?"

Two giraffes munching on leaves stopped eating and turned their heads in unison, watching Cecilia and Rocky float by.

The wind changed its mind again and they drifted toward ProctorMart. The balloon began to settle as they neared the large superstore. A big grassy meadow beckoned and Cecilia went back to the door, ready to leap out. But before they got low enough to even think about jumping, they drifted past the soft green grass and over the big black asphalt parking lot of ProctorMart, where hundreds of cars lined up in well-behaved rows.

The heat from the asphalt hit them immediately. It was as if the balloon was a soccer ball and a giant foot had kicked it upward. They shot up into the sky, so high that even the huge ProctorMart looked like a toy shop far below.

As they rose, the wind seemed to change its mind one more time. Cecilia felt the balloon start to move northward, and ProctorMart slipped from her view.

The balloon stopped rising, but the wind pushed at

them, batting them through the sky like a child playing with a toy.

The wind had made up its mind. North was the way to go.

Right toward the dire, brooding, breathing, malevolent, mist-shrouded forest of Northwood.

Cecilia gasped.

Perhaps the forest sensed she was coming. Or maybe it was just a trick of the breeze. But at that moment, two edges of the mist curled up and a gap opened in the middle. And if you looked at it a certain way and used just a little bit of imagination, you could almost say that the mist was smiling a dark and unpleasant smile.

8
THE CANOPY

THE MIST SEEMED to reach up to them as they passed over it. Cecilia pressed her fingers against the wall of the balloon.

What unknown dangers awaited them in the dark forest?

The trees, like the lake, were cold, and the balloon dropped rapidly once they were over the forest.

Cecilia looked farther to the north, hoping to see an end to the forest, praying that they might keep floating long enough to go right over the top of Northwood and emerge to farmland, or whatever was on the other side. But all she could see in that direction were trees, gesturing and grasping, dancing a macabre waltz in the gusting breeze.

They dropped farther, but so did the forest, descending

into a low valley that seemed to grow colder and darker with every foot.

They were down in the mist now. Trees stretched up with bony branches, scratching and scraping at the underside of the balloon.

Farther and farther they flew, each moment carrying them farther away from the edge of the forest. Farther away from home.

A blue bird — a kind Cecilia had never seen before — appeared alongside the balloon. It hovered for a moment as if watching them, then took off into the valley in a sudden blur of movement.

The balloon settled even lower. The scraping of the branches became louder. The balloon scuttled along on the tops of the trees, and then suddenly they were not floating anymore, but rolling and spinning along on the dense canopy that covered the forest.

Everything inside the room tumbled around — the laundry basket, the box of balloons, the helium cylinder — as did Cecilia and Rocky.

The big balloon ball rolled faster and faster along the canopy until suddenly, with a creaking of branches and a huge crash, they fell through a gap and came to a halt, wedged among the branches of an enormous black tree.

Rocky was lying on top of her. Next to Cecilia's head was the helium cylinder. She realized she was lucky not to have been hit by it as they rolled around like laundry in a clothes dryer.

Rocky got off of her, and Cecilia sat up.

"My word," she said. "Are you okay?"

Rocky was wandering around as if in a daze. He took a step, fell over, stood back up, took another step, fell over, and stood up again.

"I'm all right," he woofed. "Just a little dizzy."

Cecilia stood up and knew exactly what Rocky meant. The whole room seemed to be spinning, even though it wasn't moving at all. Shc sat down for a moment to let the dizziness pass, then looked around.

The tree that held them was not a type of tree that Cecilia recognized. The branches were thick and bulged out in strange places, like the muscular arms of a weightlifter. The leaves of the tree were not quite black, she saw, but a dark violet, and not thin like normal leaves, but thick like leather.

The blue bird they had seen before was back now, peering into the balloon before zipping away again at high speed.

After a moment, Cecilia stood up and tried to shake the

balloon free by jumping up and down, but it was firmly wedged into the branches.

"What should we do?" she said to Rocky, although she was really asking herself. "Should we stay here in the balloon or climb down into the forest?"

Rocky just raised his eyebrows. He didn't know either.

"We're probably safer in the balloon," Cecilia said, thinking it over. "In case there are any wild animals like snakes or poisonous spiders or . . ." She made herself stop. There was no point in talking like that. She didn't even know if there were any dangerous creatures in the forest. "But on the other hand, there is nothing to eat and drink here in the balloon, so we're going to have to climb down sooner or later."

A thought occurred to her and she looked up, hoping to see the sky. But all she saw were the dark leaves of the tree canopy, and above that, the mist. That meant they were hidden from above.

"Well, we can't stay here forever," she said. "So we might as well get on with it."

Rocky stared bravely at the forest around them. His nose twitched and his ears pricked up, as he tried to sense the hidden dangers. But if there were any, he could not detect them.

"Let's go," he said, with a shake of his head.

Cecilia ran her fingers through her hair. It had gotten very messy when they had tumbled over and over in the balloon. *There's no point in going off to face dark and unseen dangers if you don't look your best*, she thought.

She opened the door of the balloon, which was on its side. The door only opened part way before a tree branch stopped it.

She squeezed through the narrow gap, and climbed onto the branch.

As she did so, the balloon shifted. She was afraid that without her weight it might lift off back into the sky with Rocky inside, but the tree held it firmly.

Rocky carefully climbed out after her, and together they scrambled down. Because the branches were so thick and close together, it was almost as easy as going down a set of stairs.

There was a gap at the bottom though, and Cecilia had to jump down to the ground. Rocky stayed on the branch and whimpered at her until she persuaded him to jump.

"I'll catch you," she said, and Rocky jumped. Even though he was very light, the weight knocked Cecilia over backward and she sat down hard on her bottom with Rocky in her lap.

She quickly got back to her feet and glanced around to try to find the best way to go.

Rocky was sniffing at the ground and Cecilia saw that they were on a trail of some kind. It was the kind of trail that had been worn down by years and years of footprints. Or paw prints.

A sound came surging out of the trees like a sudden gust of wind. It reverberated through the forest, making the air around them vibrate. It was not a human sound, nor that of any animal Cecilia had ever heard before. Rocky froze in his tracks and the skin on Cecilia's head prickled.

It was a ferocious roar, rumbling from deep in the throat of some unknown creature.

9
The Clearing

THE ROAR CAME from behind them. Before Cecilia had too much time to think about it, it came again . . . closer this time.

"I think we should get going," she said quite calmly, considering the circumstances.

Rocky looked up at her and nodded.

They began to walk quickly, like a girl and a dog who were out for a walk in a forest and who were not at all terrified of some huge creature stalking them.

There was another roar, closer yet again, and they began to walk a little faster, then to run. Cecilia tried not to panic, because she once read that people who panic usually end up much worse off than they were in the first place.

The trees slipped past on either side — a thick, impenetrable wall of interlaced tree trunks and vines.

There was no way to go but forward. The path was quite smooth underfoot, except for the occasional tree root, and Cecilia tripped only once. Rocky was immediately by her side, nudging her and licking at her face as she regained her feet and stumbled forward into another run.

The smell of the forest was in her nostrils now: a dank, heavy smell of decayed plants and animal droppings.

An opening in the wall of trees appeared suddenly to their right and another to their left. Two new paths. They stopped, unsure which way to go.

Another roar and Rocky took off down the path to the right, barking back at her to follow him. Without knowing why, she trusted him, and ran after him.

The trail came to a fork, and Rocky, with a sniff in both directions, chose the left. There were more side passages in the maze of dense trees and each time Rocky seemed to know which to take.

"How do you know where to go?" Cecilia said, panting, but he just barked at her to hurry up. The path they were on came to an end at a T-junction with another, much wider trail. Rocky stopped here, confused, sniffing in both directions.

"This way," Cecilia said, pointing to the right without being sure why.

The wide path seemed well trodden and she thought she could see a clearing ahead. Something told her that the clearing was a safe place and she ran even faster with Rocky at her heels.

There was another thunderous roar from behind her and she could hear the creature, whatever it was, crashing along the path from which they had just come.

Then they were in the clearing, looking around, trying to work out what to do and where to go next. But there were high rock walls on three sides of the clearing: impenetrable cliff faces soared into the sky, with deep, shadowy crevices that peered down at them through creeping vines.

Except for the entrance to the path behind them, the fourth side of the clearing was a solid wall of black trees.

The clearing was not a place of safety, as Cecilia had thought. It was a trap.

Near the path was a round wall, a circle of stones about as high as her waist. It was very old and covered in weeds. Several of the stones were out of place or lying on the ground beside the wall. Two crumbled pillars stood at either side of the circle.

She rushed over to it, thinking they might be able to hide inside it, but all she saw was a hole in the ground,

dropping away into blackness. Her hand dislodged a small piece of stone and she heard a clunk as it bounced off the wall before landing somewhere far below with a plop.

It was a well. And that meant that people had once lived near here. But judging by the state of the well, it must have been a long time ago.

She heard another roar and glanced back up the wide trail behind them, catching a glimpse of something emerging from the side passage.

She couldn't make out its shape, black against the black trees of the forest, darkness against darkness, a huge blur in the gloom. But she sensed it turning in their direction and she began to back away slowly, knowing it was hopeless.

There was no way out of the clearing, except by the path from which they had just come. The same path that the dark creature was advancing along.

She reached out a hand and put it on Rocky next to her.

He barked and moved forward. The dog who had been afraid to get in the balloon basket, and afraid to jump down out of the balloon attic in the tree, advanced bravely to challenge the approaching nightmare.

"No," Cecilia said, knowing it was no use. One extremely thin Samoyed against a wild jungle beast.

"No," she said again, trying to control her terror.

Another sound intruded. A sliding, scraping sound. And to Cecilia's absolute astonishment, she heard a woman's voice.

"Get in here, quickly!"

10
Black Lions and Black Trees

By now there is a very good chance that you are wondering about the mysterious Northwood forest with its strange black trees and the black lions that lurk there. There is also a very good chance that you have guessed that the fearsome dark beast that was chasing Cecilia and Rocky through the forest was indeed one of those lions (which is a very good guess).

But what you don't know is what exactly the lions are, or where they came from. Neither did Cecilia.

Many years ago there were no lions in Northwood. There were no black lions, nor golden-brown ones (which is the more usual color). There were no pink lions, green lions, or purple polka-dotted lions.

No lions at all.

But now there are lions. Nobody knows how many, but

they are there, all right. Large, dangerous, beastly black lions.

Most lions have golden-brown fur, which is very useful when you are hunting for antelope or zebra on an African savanna, which is also a golden-brown color. But the black lions came from a dense jungle deep in Persia.

Few people have ever been to that jungle, and even fewer have returned. In the darkest depths of this overgrown Persian jungle, the lions' black fur is the perfect camouflage.

The lions were discovered by a famous British explorer, Sir Henry Layard. He was the first person who saw them and actually lived to tell the tale.

Even if you see a black lion and survive the encounter, you are unlikely to be able to catch the beast . . . which is why you never see black Persian lions in zoos.

So exactly how Mr. Jingles managed to capture two black lion cubs is still a mystery. But he did. He brought them back from Persia in specially made cages of hardened titanium. He knew that having such rare creatures in his safari park would make him famous around the world. He had enclosures prepared, lit by special lights and surrounded by thick glass walls, so people would be able to see the lions safely. With great care and skill, the two lion cubs (now named Prowler and Growler after a competition in the local paper) were released into their enclosure.

They stayed there just one day. The two lions escaped from their escape-proof enclosure, leaving behind crushed, crumbled glass and mangled metal bars.

They headed for the nearest jungle. The closest thing they could find was Northwood.

Prowler was a boy lion and Growler was a girl lion, and within a few years there was talk of new black lion cubs being seen at the entrance to the forest, stalking in and out of the thick wall of black trees.

Like the black lions, the tarblood trees that make up the strange forest of Northwood are very rare. With their rigid, toughened bark as hard as rock, and their sticky, tar-like sap, they are of little use to anyone. They can't be used for wood or shelter, and certainly not for decoration.

The sap, if you can drill through the outer shell and extract it, is heavy and black and burns fiercely. Yet if you touch their bark, they feel colder than normal trees, which is odd, because you would think that black trees would absorb the heat of the sun. But these trees don't.

At night, tarblood trees absorb moisture out of the air. The next day, that moisture slowly evaporates, cooling down the tree in the same way that human beings cool down by sweating. This evaporation creates a dense mist. So if you have a lot of tarblood trees growing close to each other, like in Northwood, they will always be surrounded by fog — even on a hot day.

So you see that many of the things about Northwood that seem to be quite unnatural are quite easily explained.

Northwood is really no stranger than some other peculiar things in the natural world, such as the Dumbo octopus or the giant crabs of Guam, once you know the facts.

Cecilia was about to learn these facts, and many other amazing things as well.

But it was still just the very beginning of her education. For there were things waiting to be discovered, deep in Northwood Forest, that went far beyond anything she could even dream of.

11
A Surprise Meeting

"QUICKLY!" THE WOMAN said again.

Cecilia spun around in astonishment, almost tripping over her feet, but she regained her balance just in time. A door had opened in the solid cliff face behind them. More precisely, a slab of rock with a metal post down the middle had rotated, leaving a gap on each side.

A woman stood in the opening, beckoning frantically to Cecilia and Rocky. Rocky hurled his body at the woman. Cecilia cried "No!" thinking that he was attacking her, but he just started licking her and jumping up with his paws on her chest. *His way of saying thank you,* Cecilia thought.

Cecilia followed them through the door, and it slammed shut behind them. They were in a rock-lined passageway lit by a single lantern hanging from a rusted metal hook on the wall.

"Come with me, Cecilia," the woman said. Cecilia didn't even think to ask how she knew her name. She just stood there shaking a little bit until the woman knelt down in front of her and drew her close, wrapping her arms around her and holding her tightly. Cecilia burst into tears.

It was mainly relief, Cecilia thought, now the immediate danger was past. All the worry about drifting into the forest, and her parents, and Mr. Proctor attacking her house, and everything that had happened with Rocky . . . it was all a little much, really.

She cried for what seemed like ages, but the woman did not hurry her. She just let Cecilia cry on her shoulder until the worst of the sobbing had passed. Then she handed her a small piece of cloth to dry her eyes and wipe her nose.

They followed the woman up some stairs and through more passageways, then up more stairs to a large room. Cecilia had the sense that it was a greeting room, where visitors to this place were welcomed.

There were long brass curtain rods high on the walls around the room, although any curtains they had once carried had long since rotted away. The rods themselves were green and mottled.

Cecilia sat and stared at the walls around her, her chest heaving every now and then with one of those slowpoke sobs that come long after the rest have passed. She could tell that this place was old. Very old. It was a place from times long gone. A number of doorways led out of the room, some blocked by heavy wooden doors. The wood was old and gray, cracked in places, and the brass hinges, like the curtain rods, were streaked with green.

There was a narrow window behind her, little more than a slit in the rock, and when she looked out of it she could see down into the clearing.

The creature, whatever it was, was nowhere to be seen.

The creeping vines she had seen from the clearing crawled across the open face of the window, hiding it from view, which is why she hadn't noticed it earlier. She wondered how many other levels there were in the cliff face, and how many other concealed windows.

The room reminded her of something, although it took her a few moments to realize what. It was a turret, like those in the castles in books about kings and queens and knights and princesses.

That was when she realized finally where they were, and it made her gasp and clap her hands to her cheeks.

It was a fortress cut into the face of the cliff.

She was looking out over the battlements of an ancient castle.

***

Cecilia drank a mug of something sweet that tasted like hot cocoa, but wasn't. The mug was made of a gray metal and was embossed with crossed lightning bolts.

She held the mug with one hand and kept the other on Rocky, unwilling to let him go in case he somehow disappeared. Or in case he turned out not to be real. That didn't seem very likely, but it had been a strange day. He was the only thing in this unreal world that seemed *real*.

The tall, thin woman who had made her drink returned with a bowl of water and scraps of some kind of sausage for Rocky. He sniffed at the food once and then wolfed it down, despite having had a good-sized meal only a few hours before.

The woman sat down on a wooden stool in front of Cecilia and crossed her legs, resting her hands on one knee. She stared at Cecilia.

Cecilia took another sip of the sweet, sticky drink, and looked back.

"Drink up, it'll make you feel better," the woman said.

Just those words made Cecilia feel better, because it was the sort of thing Jana would say when Cecilia was sick. It made her feel safe and a little bit at home.

"How do you know my name?" Cecilia asked. She was

sure there must be a very good reason, but was a little confused and flustered by all that had happened.

The woman leaned forward. Her face, which had been in the shadows before, was now bathed in light from the window.

"Don't you recognize me?" she asked, with a small smile that was tinged with sadness.

Cecilia's eyes opened even wider than before, if that was possible without sticky tape and Popsicle sticks. She did recognize the woman, although she was a lot thinner than when Cecilia had last seen her, and she had a different hairstyle. Cecilia realized now why Rocky had jumped all over the woman, pawing and licking, when they had first entered the castle.

"Mrs. Proctor!" Cecilia cried.

12
THE BOOK

THERE WERE SO many questions tumbling around in Cecilia's brain that they tripped over one another and none of them came out of her mouth.

She stared at Mrs. Proctor with big eyes and said nothing. There was one question that kept trying to get out, but she was afraid to ask that one because she was afraid of the answer. If she didn't ask the question, she didn't have to listen to the answer.

But it was better to face your fears, Cecilia told herself. After a few more sips, she made her mouth say the words.

"When can I go home?" she asked.

Mrs. Proctor looked at her for a moment before replying. "That's a little complicated, Cecilia."

"How complicated?" Once Cecilia had started asking, she wasn't going to stop until she found out the truth.

"Those of us who live here . . ." Mrs. Proctor trailed off. She reached out and took Cecilia's hand. "We don't live here by choice. We'd all go home if we could."

Cecilia thought that over. She knew perfectly well what Mrs. Proctor was saying, but her mind didn't want to believe it just yet. "You're trapped here?" she asked.

Mrs. Proctor nodded. "It's not a bad place to live, though. We all get along very well. I think you'll like the twins. They're about your age."

Cecilia said nothing, still getting used to the idea that she was trapped here in the dark forest.

"How did you get here?" Mrs. Proctor asked. "You didn't run away from home, did you?"

Cecilia shook her head. "There was an accident," she said. "A bulldozer smashed into our house and the attic part just floated away."

"Oh," Mrs. Proctor said as if it was the most natural thing in the world for part of a house to just lift off and float away.

"When we drifted over Northwood, we crashed into a tree and then I had to climb down."

"That was very brave," Mrs. Proctor said.

"Not really," Cecilia said. "If I had known I'd be chased by monsters, I think I would have stayed in the tree."

"Not monsters," Mrs. Proctor said, laughing. "Lions. Black lions."

"Black lions!" Cecilia said.

"Now I want to ask you a question," Mrs. Proctor said.

Cecilia nodded. "Anything."

"How is Bob — Mr. Proctor? Is he taking good care of himself? Is the store doing all right?"

Cecilia hesitated. All she could see were those sharp, spitting teeth and the horrifying yellow shape of the bulldozer as it marched toward her house. It was going to be difficult to tell Mrs. Proctor the truth.

"I think it really upset him when you disappeared," Cecilia said eventually.

"I left him a note," Mrs. Proctor said.

Cecilia nodded again. "I didn't know that. But even so, I think it really upset him. He became very angry with people. Even with me, although that was only because I stole Rocky, so I guess he had a good reason."

"You stole Rocky?" Mrs. Proctor looked at the dog, who looked back and woofed happily. "Why?"

Cecilia sighed. This was the most difficult part. "Because I didn't think Mr. Proctor was feeding him properly. I was just trying to help. I'm sorry."

Mrs. Proctor shook her head. "Don't be. Bob never

really thought much of the dog, and I can see that what you're saying is true. But please don't think too poorly of my husband. He has had a lot to deal with."

"I know," Cecilia said. She decided to tell Mrs. Proctor about the bulldozer another time.

Cecilia stood and looked out the window, staring down at the clearing in front of the castle. The whole thing seemed like a dream — one that she would have loved to wake up from — but she knew that it wasn't a dream. It was real.

"What is this place?" she asked. "Where are we?"

"Perhaps I should show you the book," replied Mrs. Proctor.

13
ORIENTATION

The Story of Princess Annachanel of Storm.

In the time before ours, during the Lost Ages, in the reign of kings and the long ride of knights, there was a castle. A fortress, built into the side of a sheer cliff at the end of a ravine. It was immensely strong and easily defended. It could not be attacked from the sides because there were none, nor from the top, because of a craggy overhang.

The castle was called Storm, and the gorge beyond it was known as Storm Gorge.

The builders, whoever they were, had constructed a network of caves that honeycombed the cliff and they dug and scraped out battlements and rooms. They built grand halls and sleeping quarters, kitchens and bathing rooms.

The castle had existed for many hundreds, maybe thousands of years. Permanent, untiring, unyielding, like the rock from which it was cut. At times it had been full of laughter and life, but now it was deserted and lonely.

To this empty castle came a young boy and girl, running for their lives, seeking a place to hide.

And the castle welcomed them in with its wide stone arms and craggy smile.

The boy, Danyon, of noble birth, and his maid, Natassia, were running from an evil landowner, the Baron of Mendoza, who had attacked their coastal town, murdering the boy's family in order to control the busy port.

More people came to Castle Storm, some running for their lives, some running from their lives. Peasants, nobles, farmers, and knights. They settled the gorge, raising crops and building farms and mills.

Time passed. The boy became a king, and the humble maid became his queen.

Danyon and Natassia ruled the castle and the gorge for many years, and the people prospered in the security and peace that it brought them.

But the Baron was not at peace. His lands were turbulent. People spoke of the missing boy. One day, they said, the boy would return at the head of an army.

The Baron was not going to wait for that to happen.

He never gave up the hunt for the missing boy. It came to pass, as these things do, that Danyon was found, and the peace of the gorge was threatened.

The Baron attacked the fortress with all the weapons at his disposal. With men in suits of hardened armor, with spears and arrows and giant wooden catapults that could throw a boulder over a thousand feet.

But the rock of the cliff was resolute and the height gave a great advantage to the defenders. Again and again, the evil troops of Baron Mendoza hurled themselves against the defenses of the castle. Boulders the size of wheelbarrows flew from the war machines, crashing against the rock. Spears and flaming arrows peppered the castle. Huge logs rammed again and again into the solid cliff face, until Danyon himself crept out under the cover of darkness and ignited prepared tar pits, burning the war machines to cinders.

The Baron withdrew, his gold depleted, but he vowed to return.

Danyon and Natassia devised a defense that no enemy could defeat. Using seeds imported from eastern lands, they planted an impenetrable maze of trees. Huge tarblood trees with black trunks as hard as rock and sap like sticky tar that would ensnare axes or saws that tried to cut them down. Natassia herself designed the devilish maze of twisting, turning, branching passageways that would draw in the unwary, trapping them in an intricate pattern from which few could escape. It took almost two decades for the trees to grow, and during that time, the Queen gave birth to a baby girl — Princess Annachanel.

When the Baron returned to the gorge, at the head of a renewed army, he found his path blocked by the huge forest. His army first attacked the trees, and then, when they realized that was futile, they attempted to find their way through the maze.

Of the four thousand men who entered, barely two hundred found their way back out, starving and emaciated, after weeks of searching for the exit.

Some of the soldiers said the trees themselves attacked them, although most thought that was simply the imagination of delirious men.

The Baron and the rest of his army were never seen again.

For the little Princess this was a wonderful, magical time. The King and Queen were adored, and although they demanded no taxes from the villagers, they were showered with gifts and love.

The ground in the gorge was fertile and food was abundant. There were celebrations and dances and great banquets at which the King and Queen would wait until all their subjects had eaten before breaking their own bread.

Amongst the villagers there were bakers, weavers, tanners, and musicians. The gorge was resplendent with deer and rabbits, and the villagers kept chickens, pigs, sheep, and cows.

The population grew and prospered and all were happy.

But time marches on relentlessly, and on a snowy winter's morning the wise King, now well into his seventies, drew his last breath. Within a year, unable to live without her great love, Queen Natassia faded away also.

The little Princess, now all grown up, became the Queen.

***

Cecilia closed the big leather-bound book with a thud of heavy pages. Dust flew out, making her nose twitch and her eyes water.

The story was just like the ones in the books she read at home, except those were all made up, and she was quite sure that this story was true.

It was written by hand in beautiful old-fashioned writing, although only the first few pages had anything on them.

The rest of the book was blank, as if the author had intended to fill it with wondrous tales of balls and banquets and great battles, but had run out of ink, or never quite found the time.

Around the room a small crowd of people was waiting expectantly for her to finish.

"But what happened to the Princess?" she asked.

"Nobody knows," Mrs. Proctor said. "The castle was deserted for many years."

Mrs. Proctor was sitting on a wooden stool by the window. The sunshine was pouring in behind her, making her sandy blond hair glow like a halo.

Next to her were Avery and Evan, the Celestine twins, who had actually been born in the forest — a fact that Cecilia was still getting used to.

Avery, a chunky, tough-looking girl, said ghoulishly, "Maybe they all died of some horrible disease."

Evan, a fine-featured boy who looked nothing like his sister, said immediately, "Don't be putrid! Where are all the bodies, or the skeletons? I bet they just moved away somewhere. Maybe they got tired of being trapped in a forest. Maybe they knew a way out."

"That's just naïve," Avery said. "I bet they all went crazy and hacked each other to pieces with axes and swords."

"That's putrid," Evan said.

"Naïve," Avery countered.

"Let Cecilia talk," Mrs. Proctor said. "I'm sure she has many more questions."

The group was a kind of a reception committee — a small group of Northwood residents who had gathered to help Cecilia adjust to life in the forest. They called it "Orientation."

"So, Cecilia," she continued, "what would you like to ask?"

"Mrs. Proctor," Cecilia asked carefully, "how did you get here? People thought you'd, um . . . left town."

"I came searching for my daughter," Mrs. Proctor said.

Cecilia looked at her in surprise.

Even Rocky, lying on the floor underneath Cecilia's legs, raised his ears.

"Jasmine?" Cecilia asked.

"Yes," Mrs. Proctor said.

A young woman on the other side of the circle raised a hand and waved. "Hi, Cecilia."

Cecilia waved back.

The girl she used to live next door to had grown up into a tall, strong-looking woman, and Cecilia barely recognized her.

Mrs. Proctor said, "It was three years ago. Jasmine was fifteen years old. It was just after Bob — that's Mr. Proctor — opened the new superstore. Jasmine got awfully angry over something, I forget what, and she ran away.

Mr. Millariquie, down at the wool store, said he saw her heading into Northwood."

On the other side of the room, Jasmine blushed and dropped her eyes, obviously embarrassed about her teenage tantrum.

Cecilia thought about that for a bit. She realized that this might have been the real reason for the sudden change in Mr. Proctor's personality after the superstore opened.

"And you came looking for her?" she asked.

"Not at first," Mrs. Proctor said. "I didn't have the courage. Nobody who goes into Northwood ever comes out. I had heard the tales of great black beasts that roamed the forest," Mrs. Proctor explained, sighing.

"But one day I could bear it no longer. I packed a bag full of food, and took along a compass and balls of string and sticks of chalk, hoping to mark my path so I could find my way back out. But the compass didn't help inside the maze, and the chalk would not write on the oily black trees. The string worked for a while, but it soon ran out, and I was lost in the maze like everyone else who had tried. I wandered for days, and finally, I saw a sign."

"A sign?" Cecilia asked.

"Yes, just a wooden arrow on a small peg stuck in the ground. I followed the arrow, which led to another arrow, and eventually I found myself here at the castle with Jasmine and the others."

"What about the lions?" Cecilia asked with wide eyes.

"I guess I was just lucky," Mrs. Proctor said. "I often heard things moving around in the distance, but they never found me in the maze. There are more lions now though, so it is much more dangerous."

Cecilia let that sink in, and then asked, "How many people live here?"

Evan jumped in to answer that one. "Thirty-nine. Forty, counting you."

"Thirty-nine!" Cecilia looked around at the other people in the reception committee.

Aside from Jasmine and the twins, the rest of them were grown-ups. She counted twelve people. The oldest was a tall, straight-backed man in his fifties who looked like a soldier. Most of their clothes appeared to be handmade with a great deal of skill and care.

"Apart from the twins, who were born here," Mrs. Proctor said, "everyone wandered in over the years, or were members of search parties for those of us who got lost here."

"And they all got past the lions?" Cecilia was a little confused.

"In the early days, there were very few lions in the forest," Jasmine said. "I heard you could walk for days and never see one, but now they seem to be everywhere."

"Thirty-nine people," Cecilia muttered.

She was still shocked at the number of people who had, for one reason or another, wandered into the black forest and never come out.

Evan was jumping up and down, itching to say something.

Mrs. Proctor smiled at him and said, "Okay, Evan."

"Here we go," Avery said, rolling her eyes.

"There are two plumbers, one mortician, four soldiers, a doctor, an electrician, a cook —"

"Who cooks the same meals over and over again," Avery interjected.

"That's not true," Evan protested.

"Yes, it is," Avery insisted.

Evan ignored her. "A bricklayer, a university professor, a teacher — that's Mrs. Proctor — and a hardware store manager. There's a priest, a butcher, a farmer, three astronomers who got lost looking for a lunar eclipse, a veterinarian, a hairdresser, a dressmaker, an accountant, two lawyers, three engineers, a cab driver, two truck drivers, a waitress, a fisherman, and a florist."

He finished and his eyes swept the room as if expecting applause.

Avery yawned loudly and significantly.

Some of those professions sounded pretty useless to Cecilia if you happened to be trapped in a castle in the middle of a deadly black forest, but she didn't say so. Instead, she blinked a couple of times while she checked the math in her head.

"But that's only thirty-five," she said after a moment. "Adults, I mean."

"It's . . . oh, plus the King, of course," Evan said.

"There's a king?" Cecilia's head suddenly filled with images of long velvet robes and golden crowns. A king! "I've never met a real king before."

A quick glance passed between Evan and Avery.

Mrs. Proctor seemed to have a strange expression on her face, but rapidly covered it with a bright smile. Then she said, "It was King Harry who went out by himself, braving the lions, to put out the arrows in the forest to guide people to safety."

"How exciting!" Cecilia said, with visions of brave King Harry striding fearlessly through the forest.

"Yeah, really," Avery said. Cecilia couldn't tell by her expression if she was serious.

Cecilia sat quietly for a moment, looking around at the rough-hewn rock walls.

"Has no one ever tried to escape?" Cecilia asked. "To find the way back through the maze?"

Mrs. Proctor nodded. "Lots of people. Lots of times. But it is too difficult and too dangerous. Nobody has ever come close to getting out."

"We made it all the way to the chimney stack rock piles," Avery said proudly, including Evan in the "we" with a sideways shift of her eyes. "Nobody had ever made it as far as that before."

"Yeah," Evan said, shaking his head. "And then we spent three days hiding in a tree and had to be rescued by Sergeant Lee. I'm not trying that again."

"I'll do it without you," Avery said defiantly, and Cecilia believed she probably would.

Most of the people in the room, including Mrs. Proctor, were either staring at the floor or slowly shaking their heads.

They had given up, Cecilia realized. They had been lost in the forest for so long that they had given up any hope of rescue or thought of escape.

A middle-aged woman whose name Cecilia had forgotten started to tell her something about the eating arrangements at the castle, but Cecilia really wasn't taking much of it in.

In the back of her mind, she was already forming a plan.

***

That night Cecilia slept in her very own bedroom with Rocky curled up at the foot of the bed. Mrs. Proctor had said Rocky could stay with her to keep her company.

"But he's your dog," Cecilia had said.

"That's okay," Mrs. Proctor said. "I can see how much he likes you. He can stay with you for a while."

Cecilia lay down on her bed, a mattress made of some kind of rough cloth and filled with straw, and stared at the dark rock ceiling of the room.

She had left the shutters open and starlight drifted in, bringing a little magic with it and filling the room with the laughter and the tears of people who had been gone for hundreds of years.

This room might have once belonged to a princess, she thought, *a beautiful little girl with diamonds in her hair and fresh flowers sewn into her gowns. Maybe even Princess Annachanel, when she was little.*

Evan said that there were exactly ninety-nine rooms in

the castle — not counting the King's quarters. (He was not allowed in there to count.)

So there were plenty of rooms for everybody, although some people, like Avery and Evan and their parents, preferred to live in one of the old stone cottages that lined the stream running through the gorge.

Cecilia loved the idea of living in the castle, even if it was quite cool and dim inside.

It was grand and old and, besides, how many ten-year-old girls actually got to live in a real castle? None that she knew!

Despite being exhausted from all her adventures that day, Cecilia still found it hard to sleep.

First, she was worried about her mother and father, because she knew they would be worried about her.

But finding her was not going to be easy.

Then she was worried about their house.

Had it collapsed after the bulldozer attack, or was it still standing? It had still been upright the last she had seen it, but it was very badly damaged.

And if she wasn't thinking about those things, then she was thinking about her plan for getting out of the forest. And that plan centered on the big attic balloon that was stuck in a tree not far from the castle.

She lay awake for a long time, listening to people walking through the corridors, talking, laughing, just living their lives.

For Cecilia, everything was brand-new . . . every experience was something she had not experienced before. So, anxious as she was, she couldn't help but be fascinated and excited at the same time.

Eventually, the corridors and the halls quieted down as people prepared for bed.

It was only after they were completely silent that she became aware of the noise.

It was a low, humming, buzzing noise and it seemed out of place in this ancient castle. It sounded like a modern kind of a noise to Cecilia.

As she finally drifted toward sleep, she resolved to ask Avery and Evan about it in the morning.

"Rocky," she asked sleepily, "how did you know the right way to come? How did you find your way here through the maze?"

Rocky rolled over on his back and itched it by rubbing it against the mattress, before answering. "I could smell people. And when we got closer, I could smell her."

Cecilia knew he meant Mrs. Proctor.

"You're very clever," she said.

"Good night," Rocky barked, which was his way of telling her to be quiet and go to sleep.

So she did, with that strange noise still humming in her ears.

14
STRAWBUBBLES

EARLY THE NEXT morning, Cecilia heard another new sound that seemed completely out of place in this ancient castle. Like a spoonful of mashed potatoes in a bowl of ice cream, it just didn't seem to belong.

She was still in bed, thinking happy thoughts, which was what she always did when she was worried about something. What was worrying her was the thought of spending weeks or months trapped in this forest-prison. So she had stopped thinking about that and instead was thinking about the lovely flower gardens that Jana kept in front of the balloon house. She hoped they hadn't been damaged when the house was attacked.

Those pretty, pretty flowers got happy, happy smiles, Jana always said.

Cecilia really missed Jana.

Cecilia was lying on her bed, thinking these thoughts, when the sound intruded. Not the buzzing/humming noise, but something completely different.

It started so faintly, she could just barely hear it. She thought at first that she must have gone back to sleep and that it was part of a dream. But the sound grew louder, and after touching herself on the nose to assure that she was wide awake, she lifted her head up so she could hear it more clearly.

It was a regular beating sound. A quiet, distant *whop whop whop*. It got louder. *WHOP WHOP WHOP.* Whatever it was, it was moving closer. And then suddenly her brain clicked into first gear and she realized what the sound was.

She rushed to the window. All she could really see was the slope of black trees on the other side of the clearing, but she could hear the sound distinctly through the mist, and it sounded very close.

Rocky jumped up with her and put his front paws on the windowsill, his ears perking up.

"It's a helicopter!" Cecilia cried. "They must be looking for us!"

She turned from the window and ran down the stairs, even as a tinny voice sounded through loudspeakers, high above the forest, echoing even over the sound of the helicopter. It was a man's voice, maybe even her father's, although it was too crackly and distant to tell.

"Cecilia."

The voice chased her down the stairs. "Cecilia Undergarment, where are you?"

By the time she burst out into the courtyard behind the castle, the sound of the helicopter was just a murmur in the distance.

Several other people were peering up at the few patches of blue sky that peeked in through the mist and the heavy branches of the trees that towered overhead from the steep sides of the gorge.

They all stayed there for a while, in case the helicopter came back, but it didn't, and they all gradually drifted back to their tasks.

***

Today, according to Mrs. Proctor, was a day of relaxation and discovery for Cecilia.

It was always the same for new arrivals. She could go anywhere (well, except the royal quarters, of course), talk to anyone, and find her way around the castle and the gorge.

Tonight would be her official welcome ceremony and

her introduction to the King. After tonight she would be expected to work.

She wasn't quite sure what her work was going to be, but she knew that everybody was expected to work hard to keep the small community running.

It might be tending to the animals (and she quite hoped it was, because she was sure they would have a lot to tell her), or it might be grinding flour or corn on the big grinding stone in the mill room.

But the thing that excited her the most was meeting the King. A real live king!

Avery and Evan were her official guides. The first three things that Cecilia learned that morning were that Avery rolled her eyes a lot, that Evan used a lot of big words but didn't really know what they meant, and that Avery and Evan argued incessantly. About anything. About everything. They argued about who was stronger (Avery) and who was smarter (Evan). About what day it was and what food was nicest and whether the sky was really blue and why water was wet and why you fell back down when you jumped in the air.

As far as Cecilia could tell, the only reason they had both volunteered to show her around was because they each didn't want the other one to be the one to do it.

They started in the courtyard. It was at the rear of the castle, cut out of the rocky plain on that side. Rocky came with them, but spent most of his time running around sniffing at things. Cecilia thought that his sensitive nose must be painting a different picture than the one she was seeing.

"From here you can see the whole valley," Evan said. "It's really esoteric."

"No you can't," Avery said.

"Well, everything except the rapids and the waterhole at the end," Evan said.

"It's not a valley," Avery said.

Avery was right. It wasn't really a valley at all. This was a gorge, or a canyon, with steep cliffs on either side that disappeared upward into the mist.

It was a deep channel across the countryside, cut millions of years ago by the river that spouted out of Storm Mountain behind them. It was not long and straight, but winding and random, zigging and zagging in odd directions as if a child had marked out the route by scrawling a jagged line on a piece of paper.

The forest of tarblood trees that now completely surrounded the gorge hid it from view, and there was only one way in or out: Storm Castle.

"That's my house," Avery said, pointing.

Scattered in groups along the banks of the river were stone cottages. Some were in quite good condition, with all four walls still standing. Others had crumbled or sunk into the earth, leaning this way and that. A number of the better-looking ones had been fixed up with doors, shutters, and roofs.

The one that Avery was pointing to was larger than the rest. It wasn't far from the castle, and it sat beside a sharp bend in the river.

Gray clothing hung from a line that went from the back of the cottage to a nearby tree, and long rows of low plants covered the ground on either side. The plants were fenced off, possibly against the goats that Cecilia could see roaming along the riverbank.

"That's *our* house," Evan said. "Not *your* house."

"It's still *my* house, even if it's also *our* house," Avery said. "What I said was correct."

"But that made it sound like it was only your house, and nobody else's," Evan said.

"I never said it wasn't your house too," Avery said.

"You implied it," Evan said.

Cecilia was feeling like telling them both to put a lid on it, but just for fun, she decided to join in instead.

"It's not a house," she said. "It's a cottage."

That immediately started off a whole new argument about whether a cottage was a type of house, or a house was a type of cottage, and what size a cottage could be before it was no longer a cottage, and whether a hut was a cottage, and what the difference between a house and a home was. On it went, and Cecilia was starting to wish she hadn't said anything.

When she could get a word in she said, "This is a lovely courtyard."

The twins stopped arguing and looked around, as if seeing the courtyard for the very first time.

There was a raised round circle with a roof at one end. Cecilia thought it was a place where minstrels might have played once, while citizens, wearing fine robes and elegant gowns, waltzed joyfully around the courtyard.

A small stream, diverted from the main river, gurgled its way across the courtyard through a channel made of stones.

The stream ran into a water feature in the middle of the courtyard: a rock-lined waterfall that flowed in a constant sheet of water into a large open bowl on a lower level.

In the middle of the bowl, on a raised pedestal, was a

birdbath. In the center of the birdbath was a little golden statue of a bird.

A blue bird was taking a bath. "Hello, pretty little bird," Cecilia said, keeping one hand on Rocky's collar in case he should take off and try to chase it.

"It's okay," Rocky woofed. "I'm not hungry."

Cecilia kept her hand on his collar anyway, because she knew that dogs did not always tell the truth, especially when it came to chasing cats and birds.

"Hello, blue bird," she said again.

The bird turned its head each way, as birds do to get a good look at you.

Cecilia didn't expect the bird to say anything back. She had found that birds didn't talk very much and what they did say was usually not worth saying.

This blue bird gave a quick chirp that might have meant, *Do you mind? I'm taking a bath.*

Looking back to the gorge, she saw why her eyes had been drawn straightaway to the blue bird.

The constant mist that covered the narrow gorge, from the tarblood trees on top of the cliffs on either side, sucked all the color out of everything.

It was all quite dull and lifeless: the lazy water of the river, the grass and reeds along the riverbanks, the simple smocks the people wore, the stone houses, even the gold of the little bird statue. Everything looked gray.

The trees themselves were black, and the mist was white. It seemed that everything else was some shade in between. It was as if she had gone from a color-TV world to a black-and-white one. Except for the blue bird — its vibrant feathers were the single splash of color in this dull, overcast place.

The twins showed her many of the important rooms in the castle. There was the pottery room, where they made clay pots for water and smaller, flatter pots for what Avery called "night water." (Cecilia knew they were actually little toilets.) The potter, Mrs. Armishaw (a former astronomer), also made mugs and plates and vases.

In another room, the weaver, Mr. Herald (the former accountant), made cloth out of wool and some coarse threads they took from one of the bushes in the gorge. She met the furrier (the former hairdresser), Mr. Kent, who had rabbit skins stretched on frames, and the baker (also an astronomer), his face red and sweaty.

She tried to remember all the names, and what they did, but she knew it would take a couple of days before it all sank in.

She and the twins ended up back in the courtyard.

"Come and see our farm," Evan said.

"Farmlet," Avery said.

"Whatever," Evan said.

They started walking down the huge steps.

"Last night I heard a strange sound," Cecilia said. "It was like a buzz or a hum, and it seemed to go on all night. What was that?"

"The castle ghost," Evan said immediately.

"There are no such things as ghosts," Avery said.

"Just because you've never seen one doesn't mean they aren't there," Evan said. "It's a polterghost."

"Do you mean a *poltergeist*?" Cecilia asked.

"No, it's definitely a ghost," Evan said.

"He's an idiot," Avery said to Cecilia. "Nobody really knows what it is. Only kids can hear it, because our ears are better than grown-up ears."

"It's the ghost of King Danyon, humming to himself," Evan said.

"It's not a very catchy tune," Cecilia said.

"I think it's an underground river," Avery said. "It flows up inside the mountain and comes out at the riverhead spring. The humming is the noise of the water rushing through the rock."

"It doesn't sound like water," Evan said.

"And you're an expert on underground rivers?" asked Avery.

"What do you grow on your farm?" Cecilia asked, hoping to change the subject.

"Farmlet," Avery said.

"Strawbubbles," Evan said.

Cecilia frowned.

"Do you mean strawberries?" she asked.

"No, they're much better than strawberries," Evan said.

"How would you know? You've never eaten a strawberry," Avery said.

"Mom says they're better," Evan said.

"What are they?" Cecilia asked.

"They're like strawberries," Evan said.

Seeing his sister's expression, he added, "Mom says. But they're sweeter and full of little pockets of air, so they're really fun to eat."

"They only grow here in Storm Gorge, Mom says," Evan continued. "There are lots of plants that have grown here for thousands of years, but they don't grow anywhere else in the world."

"Wow." Cecilia's eyes sparkled at the thought of all these new things to learn.

"What kinds of things grow here?"

"Well," Avery said, "there are burgerberries, applets, crawling beans, catichokes —"

Evan jumped in. "Gobbage, oilives, graperoot, and giant sneezeweed."

"Eww," Cecilia said. "That doesn't sound very good."

"Sneezeweed?" Evan said, looking a little surprised. "It's yummy! You stew it and serve it with cream. Ordinary sneezeweed can be a little bitter, but giant sneezeweed is delicious."

"I don't like it," Avery muttered.

By this time they had reached the twins' cottage. Evan insisted Cecilia try a strawbubble.

"They're perfect," he said. "Just ripe. Tomorrow we start the harvest."

Cecilia took the strawbubble that Evan picked off the low vine.

She tentatively nibbled at one end.

"No, no," Avery said. "You have to put the whole thing in, like this."

She picked another one off the vine, pulled out the green stalk, and put the berry into her mouth.

Cecilia did the same.

It does taste a little like a strawberry, she thought, *but it fizzes in my mouth like a soft drink.* It was the most extraordinary sensation.

"They're delicious!" she exclaimed.

A bony-looking woman was tending the vines at the back of the strawbubble field. She looked over and waved, and Cecilia waved back.

Avery said, "That's Mom. You can meet her later. There are lots more things to show you."

Cecilia was dying to tell Avery and Evan about her plan, but she decided to wait until that night, so she could tell the King first.

Two men walked past them, heading toward a beech forest that covered both sides of the riverbanks a little farther downstream. They had bows and arrows slung over their shoulders.

"Jack and Jerry," Avery said. "They're our hunters."

"They're really good," Evan said. "They can hit a target three hundred feet away."

"When I grow up I want to be a hunter," Avery said.

"You'd be useless," Evan said.

"I'd be better than you," Avery said.

The hunters smiled and waved at Cecilia.

Past the twins' house she saw a fisherman waist-deep in the river checking his nets.

She watched him for a while and a warm glow washed over her. She was surprisingly happy in this strange, old-fashioned world.

15
THE HAPPY HIPPY

CECILIA COULDN'T WAIT to meet the King and tell him her idea.

She waited patiently with the others in the throne room. It was a grand hall deep in the castle. It looked like it might have once been a large cave and had been extended by the original builders of the castle.

The throne itself was very impressive, carved from the rear wall of the room and patterned with ornate designs of clouds and birds. In the center were the two crossed lightning bolts she had seen on the mug. These bolts were made of gold and they glittered in the light from the lanterns that lined the walls.

There was a kind of a trumpeting sound, which was really just old Gimpy, the court musician, blowing raspberries into a hollow tube of wood. Next, four large men entered, in two rows of two. One of the leading guards, a big bearlike man, called out in a pompous voice, "All hail the King."

"Long live the King," everybody else chorused, except for Cecilia who hadn't known what was expected.

"All hail the King," the guard called out again.

This time Cecilia joined in. "Long live the King!"

Once more he called it out, and once more they repeated the answer.

Cecilia was starting to worry that this might go on all night, but then the King came striding into the room.

Cecilia's first thought when she saw him was that he didn't look like a king at all. At least not like the kings in picture books. Those kings were always wise and regal, and usually quite handsome too, with a short beard or a goatee. And they were usually tall and wore long, flowing robes and a golden crown.

The only thing about the King of Storm that matched that description was that he wore a crown — a large golden one that glittered with jewels. Her heart beat faster when she saw it. But the great man himself was quite a disappointment for a girl who had been brought up on tales of King Arthur.

To begin with, he wasn't very tall. In fact, he wasn't

that much taller than Cecilia. And he was quite round, if it can be put that way politely. This was strange because all the other residents of Storm were thin from working hard and always having only just enough to eat.

He didn't wear long, flowing robes either — quite the opposite. He wore short pants and leather sandals, and his hairy little legs looked to Cecilia like two furry otters crawling up poles.

His top half was covered — well, almost covered — by a shapeless shirt with long sleeves and tassels. The shirt was multicolored, with overlapping circles that made Cecilia's eyes water if she gazed at them too long. It wasn't quite long enough to cover his round stomach, which was also hairy and stuck out at the bottom of the shirt. Cecilia did not think this was a pretty sight, but was careful not to show this on her face.

His hair was long and held back in a ponytail. His beard was just as long and also tied in a ponytail.

He was a most unique-looking gentleman. When Cecilia thought about it, she realized he looked like the hippies from the 1960s that she had seen pictures of in books . . . except he was a king.

His name was King Harry.

Well, officially his name was Harold the Merciful, King

of Storm and all its Environs, but nobody ever called him that and he had given up trying to get them to.

So most people just called him King Harry, or King for short. Except for Avery who called him King Hairy the Marsupial, but not to his face.

King Harry sat on the carved rock throne. Well, let's be honest — he hopped up onto the throne, which was much too high for him, and wiggled his wobbly bottom backward until he was sitting squarely. His feet stuck straight out in the air in front of him. They were hairy, too, and not very clean. He took a handful of nuts from a bowl, stuffing them into his mouth.

Mrs. Proctor stepped forward. "Your Highness. May I present to you your newest loyal subject, Ms. Cecilia Undergarment, formerly of Brookfield."

King Harry gave her a crunchy smile. "Come forward, little one."

Cecilia strode obediently forward, although she didn't really like being called little one, especially by an adult who was not much taller than she was. But she didn't say anything. He was the King, after all.

Guards sat on either side of him. They seemed quite tough, and not particularly friendly — especially the man closest to the King, who looked like a big, growly bear.

Evan had told her the guards were soldiers, part of a huge rescue party sent in after the three astronomers had gone missing.

Cecilia approached the throne and bowed her head, as one should always do when meeting a king.

King Harry seemed quite pleased with that gesture.

"Welcome to Storm," he said in a booming voice, and his smile widened. "I am happy to meet thee. I trust thou hast been treated well."

The way he said "thou" and "hast" sounded quite silly, Cecilia thought. It was as if he was trying to sound royal by saying old-fashioned words.

"Yes, very well," she said brightly. "May I also say —"

She stopped, seeing the looks on the guards' faces and hearing the drawing in of breath from around the room.

"No," the King said, shaking his head. "No thou may not."

One of the guards, who looked a little like a weasel, pointed a finger at Cecilia and said, "Speak only when spoken to, and if asked a question, just answer it."

She nodded, a little frightened, and glanced at Mrs. Proctor, who kept her face expressionless.

"Thou may kiss the royal hand," King Harry said, extending that royal hand out in front of him, palm down.

Cecilia peered at his hand. It was just as hairy as the rest of him, and not particularly clean, and certainly not very royal.

"That's okay. Thanks anyway," she said.

"It wasn't a suggestion; it was a royal command," growled the big bear guard.

"I'd really rather not," Cecilia said, trying not to let her nose turn up at the slightly unkempt paw.

From the frowns on the guards' faces, and the horrified looks around the room, it was pretty clear to Cecilia that this was not the way to talk to a king — not *this* king at least.

"Do it or I'll make you do it," the big bear guard said in a low rasp.

"Make me? What are you going to do?" she asked, starting to get angry. "Throw me in a dungeon? I'm only ten. That wouldn't be very nice. I'm sure the King is a wise and benevolent ruler who would never let you do something like that," she finished.

Those were words she had often read in her books about kings and queens, and she guessed, correctly, that King Harry would be pleased to hear them.

Two of the guards, including the big bear man, rose up out of their seats, but King Hairy the Marsupial raised a hand to stop them. He sat up a little straighter in his chair and brushed some imaginary fluff off one sleeve.

"Wise and benevolent," he said, rolling the words around in his mouth. "Thou art a good judge of people, my dear, and of course I would never send a small child to the dungeons." He sounded sincere, although there was a flash of something in his eye that made Cecilia wonder if he was telling the truth.

"On this occasion, as thou art new," the King said, "thou will be excused for thine insult to thy King. I am not only wise and benevolent, but I am also Harry the *Merciful.*"

Cecilia looked around in time to see Avery do one of her famous eye rolls.

King Harry continued. "But in the future, thou will respect the laws and rules of Storm. The only way a community can live together peacefully is by having rules that everybody follows — the small rules as well as the big rules."

"Well actually, I don't really intend to live here," Cecilia said. "I have been thinking about how we might be able to get out of here, and I have come up with quite a good plan."

16
Cecilia's Plan

"A PLAN?" KING HARRY sounded excited. Or was he just being sarcastic? Cecilia couldn't be sure. She didn't like people who were sarcastic. "A plan?!" King Harry sat back in his chair and pressed his fingertips together, raising his eyebrows at the same time. Now Cecilia was quite sure he was being sarcastic. "A ten-year-old girl, a chick barely out of her nest, on just her second day in Storm, hath come up with a plan?"

The big beary guard snorted, and the others laughed.

Around the rest of the room there was silence.

"Yes, I really have," Cecilia said. "Would you like to hear it?"

"Would I like to hear thy plan?" King Harry was playing to an audience, although most of them didn't appear very impressed with his acting. "Why would I not want to hear a plan from such a little chick, when all the rest of us, who have been racking our brains for years looking for a way to escape, could not think of anything? Nay, on second thought, I do not desire to heareth of your plan."

"Maybe some of the others do," Cecilia said in a small but determined voice.

"No doubt!" King Harry thundered. "Why would they not? Who here would like to hear a little chick show us all how stupid we are?"

King Harry, who by now Cecilia quite disliked, opened his mouth to speak again, but before he could do so, a voice intruded.

"Actually, I would." It was Avery.

There was a stunned silence. Cecilia saw a quick glance flick from the King to the burly bearlike guard. The next thing Cecilia knew, the guard was over by Avery, grabbing her by the ear and dragging her to the center of the room.

"I would too," Mrs. Proctor said.

"Let her speak," the twins' mother said, although it earned her a warning glance from her husband.

The guard let go of Avery's ear and turned to look at her, but there was a chorus of murmurs around the room and lots of nodding. King Harry shut his mouth. All the words he was about to say must have got caught in his

throat, because his face turned quite red and looked like it was swelling up and might pop.

"Then let us hear thy 'plan,'" he said finally. "After all, I am a wise and benevolent king, and a wise king will always listen to the advice of others."

Saying you are wise and benevolent doesn't make it true, Cecilia thought.

Avery quietly slipped back to her place, rubbing her ear and scowling at the guard.

"Well," Cecilia began. "First, I don't for a moment think that I am more clever than any of you. Especially you, Your Royal Highness."

That small piece of flattery seemed to mollify the King somewhat, because he relaxed a little in his throne and indicated with a wave of a finger that she should continue.

"But I didn't walk here, through the forest, through the maze, like most of you did. I flew here in a helium balloon, which is now lodged in a tree not far from the castle."

There were some gasps of astonishment from the crowd.

"A balloon," somebody whispered loudly.

"It got loose accidentally," Cecilia said, being careful not to look at Mrs. Proctor. "And the wind blew me into the forest."

"Thou cannot expect to put every one of us in a balloon and fly us out," King Harry said. "There are far too many of us. That is the most stupid . . ."

"No, that's not it," Cecilia said, feeling quite proud of herself. "You all saw or heard that helicopter flying around yesterday. They were looking for me. My daddy is really rich, and he could hire a helicopter for weeks to keep searching if he thought there was a chance of finding me."

"He's probably happy to see you go, you know-it-all little brat," she heard the King mutter under his breath.

Cecilia didn't let it stop her.

"Inside that big balloon there's a box of smaller balloons and a tank of helium gas. We could go and get them, bring them back to the castle, inflate a bunch of the balloons and tie them to a long rope. Maybe in the courtyard. Then we could let it float up into the sky above the trees and the mist. It would be like a beacon. It could signal to the helicopter, or any planes that fly overhead, to let them know where we are."

She finished proudly and saw many wide eyes and the beginnings of smiles. *It's a very clever idea,* she thought. There was a strange electricity in the room and Cecilia recognized it immediately. *Hope.*

She turned back to King Harry to find him nodding.

"Indeed I am surprised. That is a good plan, little chick," he said. "Art thou sure thou would be able to find thy way back to this balloon of yours?" Cecilia thought about that. There had been a lot of twists and turns, and a black lion had been chasing them.

"I can find it," Rocky woofed, sitting next to Mrs. Proctor.

King Harry looked at him, noticing the dog for the first time. "Whose dog is this?" he asked. "I do not allow dogs in my throne room."

"It's my dog," Mrs. Proctor said. "But he seems to have taken quite a liking to Cecilia."

King Harry stared at Rocky for a moment, then back at Cecilia, apparently deciding not to start another argument.

"I was asking if thou could find this balloon of thine," he asked.

"Yes, I think so," Cecilia said.

"But art thou sure, little chick?"

Cecilia thought that if the King called her a little chick one more time she would set fire to his beard. But she swallowed that thought.

"Am I sure I can find it?" she asked, as if to herself, but she was looking straight at Rocky.

Rocky nodded, but pretended to be scratching his ear so nobody would notice.

"Yes, I'm quite positive," she said.

"Well then, that makes it a matter of some rejoicing," King Harry said. "All our problems are solved."

"We should go soon," Cecilia said. "The sooner we fly the balloons, the sooner they can find us."

King Harry shook his head. "It will take us a day to prepare the rope, and tomorrow we start the spring harvest. We need every hand to help us bring it in. So it will have to wait until next week."

"Next week!" Cecilia exclaimed. "But if we get rescued, you won't need your spring harvest. We can all dine out at Longfellow's restaurant and buy groceries from ProctorMart."

"And if thy plan does not work, and we do not get rescued? How will we survive next winter without our spring harvest safely in the storerooms? We will starve, and it will be thy fault!" He glared at her as if she was responsible for something that hadn't even happened yet.

"But if we wait for a whole week, the helicopter might be gone. They might have given up!"

"Aha!" King Harry pounced on her words. "Thou said

thy father was so rich that he would hire a helicopter for weeks. So they will still be searching. We can bring in our harvest, just in case, and then fly thy balloons, and if it all works and we get rescued it will have only cost us a week."

"Yes, but . . ." Cecilia trailed off, realizing that she was not going to win. In her heart she knew that if they waited a week, it would be too late. The helicopter was searching *now.* In a week they would probably have given up and moved on to some other part of the huge forest.

"Then it is decided," King Harry proclaimed from his throne. "We will bring in the harvest, then go look for the girl's balloon." He clapped his hands together twice. "Let us now adjourn for the welcome feast."

Several people disappeared and returned with huge plates of food, which they placed on the long central table that ran down the great hall.

It smelled good, but Cecilia found she wasn't feeling very hungry.

17
JAZZ

THE NEXT DAY, as decreed, Cecilia started work. Not with the animals, as she had hoped, but in the mill room, helping Jasmine Proctor grind grain to make bread.

Nobody except her mother called her Jasmine, Cecilia discovered. To everyone else, she was simply Jazz.

It was harder work than Cecilia thought, and quite boring. But when she thought about it, she figured most of the jobs in this world probably were hard and boring.

In fact, life itself was quite boring. There was no TV to watch and no computer games to play. Not even solitaire. There were no books to read besides the one about Princess Annachanel, and that was just two pages long.

Even if they had a TV, there would be no time to watch it. Every day, except Sunday, everybody had to work.

With only forty people (including Cecilia), it was a

constant battle to get all the jobs done that were needed to provide food and shelter for the community. Today, Cecilia's job was to pour the grains into a big brass funnel that was on the top of the stone mill. It was tall, so she had to stand on a wooden stool to reach it.

There were two stones in the mill: a bottom one that didn't move and a top one that rotated around. It was driven by some gears and a long wooden pole that went out through a hole in the wall to turn a water mill outside.

Somehow the grains she was pouring were pulled through the two stones, getting ground into a fine powder, then sifted out into a big round dish. Jazz would scoop up the ground flour and put it into small cloth sacks.

Cecilia watched Jazz working. She scraped out the flour from around the stone with quick, easy movements. Jazz was slender and willowy, with a slightly turned up nose and a hint of mystery in her eyes. Cecilia imagined that in Brookfield there would have been a bunch of young men hanging around her wherever she went.

Jazz saw her looking and smiled. "You're very brave," she said, "standing up to the King like that."

"Brave?" Cecilia was surprised. "I really didn't think I was being brave. Actually, I thought I was being kind of rude, but that was because I got a little angry."

"It was fun to watch." Jazz's smile turned into a huge grin. "Everyone else is terrified of the King, so we all enjoyed seeing him squirm because of a ten-year-old girl."

"A good king wouldn't terrify his subjects. He would earn their respect," Cecilia said.

"You're right," Jazz said. "That is what a good king would do."

"To be honest I really didn't like him very much," Cecilia said. "But I don't know him yet. I should give him a chance before I make up my mind about him."

Jazz laughed. "You're a little ray of sunshine, you are."

"Why did you run away?" Cecilia asked, shoveling another load of grains, climbing up on the stool, and tipping it into the funnel.

The laughter disappeared. Jazz folded down the top of another full sack of flour and looked at her.

"It was nothing," she said. "It was just stupid. I don't even really remember what started the argument. I guess Father was under a lot of pressure, and I was just having a really bad day."

"But why did you come here?" Cecilia asked.

"I didn't mean to," Jazz replied. "I just stormed out and said I was never coming back, and the next thing I knew, I was walking into the forest. I didn't know what I was doing and I really didn't care what happened to me. That was then. And now . . ."

She stopped talking and gestured at the grindstone, then reached down to scoop up some more flour.

Cecilia opened her mouth to ask another question, but closed it again, seeing the single tear that was making a small path through the fine layer of flour on Jazz's cheek.

A tiny streak of sunlight somehow snuck in through a gap in the misty tree canopy above and found its way into the mill room. The tear flashed for a moment before Jazz wiped it away with a dusty wrist.

But that tiny flash made Cecilia's heart go quiet and still.

It made her think of all the things that Jazz was missing outside of the forest — all the things that the other girls her age were doing. Driving lessons and school graduations. Drooling over photos of favorite movie stars while listening to favorite bands. Giggling with her friends at parties.

And it wasn't just Jazz who would be missing out on those things.

Unless her plan succeeded, so would Cecilia.

***

Cecilia had started work at seven in the morning, right after breakfast, and finished at four in the afternoon. It was a long day and her arms ached at the end of it, but Jazz's job was much harder than hers and she never once complained.

Everyone else was involved in the harvest, even David Ovink, the usual grain-pourer, which was why Cecilia had been given that job.

There were only a few jobs that had to go on every day, regardless of the harvest, and grinding the grain was one of them.

When she finished, despite her exhaustion, she raced straight over to the twins' house, but found them halfway there, lying on the riverbank with their toes in the water, arguing.

"I hate picking crawling beans," Evan was saying. "They go everywhere. I had three crawl up inside my shirt today. They give me the chills."

"Better than being up to your waist in mud, picking gobbage," Avery said.

Both of them were streaked with sweat and dust, and barely had the energy to raise their heads when Cecilia arrived.

"Hi, Avery. Hi, Evan," Cecilia said, plonking herself

down beside them and taking off her shoes and socks so she could dangle her toes in the river also.

The water was cold, but soothing for her poor feet, which had been working very hard to hold her up all day long.

"Hi, Cecilia," Avery said.

"How was your day in the mill?" Evan asked.

"It was okay," Cecilia said. "Jazz is nice."

"She's a snob," Avery said. "She never talks to me."

"No she's not," Evan said. "She's just shy."

"I think she's mostly sad," Cecilia said.

Evan and Avery thought that over for a moment as the river strolled past, tickling their toes as it went.

"I loved your idea about the balloons," Evan said.

"You didn't even know what a balloon was," Avery said. "You had to ask Mom."

"Neither did you."

"I did so!"

"I'm really worried about it," Cecilia said, interrupting them. "I'm afraid that they will have stopped searching in a week."

"But you said your father could afford to keep searching for weeks," Avery said.

"You told the King," Evan said, agreeing with his sister for once.

"I know what I said," Cecilia said. "But what if I'm wrong? Then we could fly the balloons all day long and it wouldn't do any good."

"You won't be able to change his mind," Avery said. "Not now that the harvest has started."

Evan said nothing. He was just looking at Cecilia and she had the distinct impression that he was reading her mind.

"You don't want to wait, do you?" he said. "You want to sneak out and try to do it by yourself."

A group of workers was making their way back up the river from the harvest, sacks full of something hoisted over their shoulders. Cecilia stopped talking as they came within earshot.

The man at the front of the group was huge — even taller than the grizzly bear guard. His shoulders were wide like the stones in the mill, and his chest was a big barrel full of muscle.

"Who's that?" Cecilia asked.

"That's just Tony," Evan said.

"Tony Baloney," Avery added. "He's our tar man. He

collects the tar that we burn for lights and cooking and everything."

"He used to be a bricklayer," Evan said, "but we don't have bricks here."

He must have laid a lot of bricks back in the real world, Cecilia thought, looking at those huge shoulders.

"He helped us fix up our cottage," Evan said. "He helped fix most of them."

All the others in the group were struggling under the weight of their heavy sacks, and could barely muster enough breath to say hello as they neared.

Tony Baloney, however, had not one, but two sacks hoisted over his shoulder, and he carried them as if they were full of nothing but balloons.

Every now and then as he walked he would beat his chest with his free hand, and holler out to nobody, "Boomphah!"

Cecilia and the twins watched the group approach.

"Boomphah!"

"Boomphah!"

"Boomphah, boomphah, boomphah!"

Tony gave Cecilia such a huge smile that she couldn't help but grin back.

He held out his free hand toward her, acting like King

Harry asking for the royal hand kiss, then he shook his head with an expression of disgust and burst into laughter.

"What are you going to do, throw me in a dungeon?" one of the others in the group said, and they all laughed.

"You're a legend around here already," Avery said.

"Nobody has ever dared stand up to the King like that," Evan added.

The group disappeared up toward the castle, still laughing.

Tony Baloney looked back over his shoulder and shouted, "Boomphah!"

Cecilia smiled and waved goodbye.

Both of the twins were grinning too. *There is something about Tony that makes you smile,* Cecilia thought. She liked him right away.

"What's with the 'Boomphah?'" she asked.

Avery touched her ear and then her mouth, and shook her head. "He can't hear or speak," she said.

"And he's not the smartest rock in the river," Evan said.

"You don't know that." Avery punched her brother on the arm. "Don't be mean. Just because he can't speak doesn't mean he's stupid."

She turned back to Cecilia. "That whole hitting his chest thing and shouting — Mom says he can feel the vibrations and he likes the way his mouth feels when he yells it out. He does it when he's happy."

"I like him," Cecilia said.

"Everybody does," Evan said.

"Anyway," Avery said. "What's this idea about sneaking out and trying to float the balloons?"

Cecilia took a deep breath. "Well, if the King won't help, then I'll just have to do it myself."

"We'll help you," Avery said.

"No we won't," Evan said.

"Don't worry about him," Avery said. "We'll help."

"It's too dangerous," Evan said.

"We'll go at night — when the lions are sleeping," Avery said.

Cecilia was surprised. "Do the lions sleep at night?"

Avery nodded.

"But they wake up really fast if they hear you moving along the paths," Evan said. "And at night you can't see them coming, so they're even more precarious."

"Oh." Cecilia wasn't sure it was a good idea after all.

"Don't worry about it." Avery said, grinning. "We'll just have to be really quiet, that's all. Are you sure you can find the landing place?"

"I'm sure we can find it," Cecilia said, meaning her and Rocky, so it wasn't a lie. "What about the rope?"

"That won't be a problem," Avery said.

"We're not going," Evan said.

"Yes we are," Avery said.

In fights like this one, Cecilia had discovered, it was usually Avery who won.

18
THE EXPEDITION

EVERY DAY THEY waited was a wasted day, Cecilia felt. So even though she was exhausted from the day's work in the mill room, the expedition had to be that night right after dinner.

Everyone in Northwood had dinner together in the big castle banquet hall. That night it was burgerberry burgers. They were delicious, Cecilia thought, and quite filling.

They were made with bread rolls from the bakery, fresh sandyleaf salad, ordinary-looking tomatoes, and patties made from burgerberries, which turned out to be something like soybeans. The chefs mashed them up and added some other ingredients and fried them on the big stove tops.

Afterward there was strawbubble shortcake for dessert. Yum!

***

She met up with the Celestine twins again right after dinner. It was already dark and the rock walls of the castle flickered under the soft glow of the lanterns on the walls. Rocky trotted along beside them. He had spent the day with Mrs. Proctor, since he wasn't allowed in the mill room for hygiene reasons.

Avery had a long coil of rope over her shoulder. "There was plenty of rope in the storeroom," she said, "and King Hairy was just being a liar when he said it would take a day to get it ready."

They found their way to the greeting room, being careful that nobody saw them — especially the four guards.

The twins had names for all the guards, Cecilia discovered. The big, bearlike man was Grizzly. Then there was Wolf, Weasel, and Skunk.

Evan called them King Harry's private zoo.

From the greeting room they surveyed the clearing to make sure there were no lions sleeping below.

"How would we even know?" Cecilia asked. "It's too dark to see anything."

"Just listen," Evan said. "They snore."

"And if the snoring stops . . ." Avery added, ". . . run."

They listened intently, but all Cecilia could hear was

the low throbbing hum of the underground river, or the ghost of King Danyon, or whatever it was.

The twins also seemed satisfied, although Evan grumbled a couple of times about how dangerous it was.

"What if one of the lions is awake?" Cecilia asked.

"Yeah, an insomnomaniac lion," Evan said.

"They'll be asleep," Avery said firmly.

The corridor with the big stone door was unlit, but Avery took a lantern off a hook on the wall and clicked something a couple of times until it produced a strong orange glow. They unlocked the door by lifting three heavy wooden braces off of some large hooks. Evan and Cecilia took one end of each brace and Avery took the other end all by herself. They stacked the braces by the door and Cecilia picked up the lantern while Avery and Evan heaved on the door to open it, swiveling it around on its central hinge. They pushed it shut again once they were through.

"How will we get back in?" Cecilia asked, looking at the blank face of the cliff. When the door was shut it fitted so seamlessly into the rock face that it was completely invisible.

"We just push on the other side of the door," Avery said. "On the left side. Then it will swivel and open just like before."

"As long as nobody has replaced the braces," Evan said.

"Worrywart," Avery said.

"Daredevil," Evan said.

"I thought we were supposed to be quiet," Cecilia said, which shut them both up quickly.

They were alone in the clearing, with the cliff face towering above them and just a cool breeze whispering through the tarblood trees for company.

It reminded Cecilia of her first day in the forest, and she shuddered.

They crept forward under the stars, which were bright and clear above them. Unlike during the day, there was no mist.

We are just like King Danyon sneaking out to set fire to the catapults, Cecilia thought, seeing it all in her imagination. The dark mounds of the sleeping soldiers littering the ground in front of her. The giant wooden war machines towering above the trees in the distance. Creeping along silently in the darkness, knowing that it would just take one alert soldier and you were dead. A curious thought occurred to her just at that moment, but she tucked it away for later. There was other business at hand.

Rocky led them straight to the wide pathway and sniffed at it. He looked back at Cecilia and gave her a quiet woof to say there were no lions nearby, and that he would smell them if there were.

She nodded to let him know she understood.

Rocky put his nose to the ground and started walking, following their scent from a couple of days ago. Cecilia followed behind with the lantern, which cast slivers of burnt orange light out into the murky crevices of the forest.

By day, the forest was dark and creepy. By night, it was a scene from a nightmare. The trees seemed to grow and shrink as the lantern moved past them. The muscular branches reached out for them, seeking their throats with spindly fingers, only to draw back at the last moment.

At each path they came to, Rocky, with a quick sniff, knew exactly which way to go. Without him, Cecilia realized, they would have had no chance of finding the balloon.

Each trail looked exactly the same to her, and so when Rocky suddenly came to a halt in the middle of a path, she could not understand why.

"What's happening, Rocky?" she asked. "Why did we stop? Is this the place?"

Looking up in the trees around them, she could see no sign of the big attic balloon.

"Lion," Rocky woofed.

"How close?" Cecilia whispered as quietly as she could.

"I'm not sure," Rocky said.

"It's like you're talking to that dog," Avery said.

Cecilia laughed quickly and said, "I think there may be a lion nearby."

They listened for a moment, but heard nothing.

"Let's keep going, but be really quiet," Cecilia said, more bravely than she felt.

Another twenty feet down the trail, they heard it — a faint snoring sound. It grew louder with each step and so did the pounding of the blood in Cecilia's ears.

It wasn't really a snoring sound at all, but she could see why they called it that. It was more like a loud, rhythmical purring, as the big cat breathed in and out in its sleep.

A little farther and Rocky stopped again. The purring/snoring was loud here, and Cecilia knew the lion must be close.

As long as it keeps snoring, we're okay, she thought.

Rocky was looking upward and pawing silently at the base of one of the trees. *This is the tree we crashed into!* Cecilia realized.

She gestured to Evan to hold the light for a moment and clambered up onto a heavy root that looked like the leg of an ogre. She found a branch and pulled herself up, then reached back down for the lantern.

Peering up, she could see nothing. She was just starting to wonder if this was the right tree after all when she noticed the little patch of green lying on one of the branches. It was flat and lifeless — a green balloon. One of the balloons from the attic. It was lying in the elbow of one of the branches of the tree and had obviously fallen out when they had opened the door.

This *was* the tree, all right.

But the attic balloon was gone.

Looking now, she could see where the balloon had landed, trapped in a fork of heavy branches.

The balloon must have worked itself free in the breeze and floated away.

All her plans went floating away into the sky with it — her brilliant idea, her chance to save the people of Storm and lead them back to civilization.

She noticed something else: a small scrap of fabric caught on a jagged branch. She tried to grab it, but it was just out of reach. She stretched up onto tippy-toes, and her fingers closed over it just as her foot slipped.

She scrambled around wildly for balance, trying to clutch onto something, anything, but all she caught was thin air. Stifling a sharp cry that tried to force its way from her throat, she slid back down the bulbous trunk of the tree and landed with a thump on the ground. The lantern landed next to her with a thud and went out.

Then the snoring stopped.

19
The Well

IT WAS PITCH black.

"We need to get out of here," Evan whispered.

"Hang on a minute," Avery said.

"Why?" Evan's voice was a tight croak.

"Because we don't know where it is," Avery hissed. "We could end up running right toward it. Just listen for a second."

They all listened.

The lion was very close . . . so close they could hear it breathing, even now that it was awake.

They could hear the lion's footsteps padding on the leaves underfoot and then there was a low growl from its throat.

"It sounds like it's right beside us," Cecilia said, trying not to panic.

"It is," Avery said.

There were some clicking sounds and the lantern burst back into life in Avery's hands.

Rocky was staring straight at the trees on the other side of the path.

"It's there," he woofed.

Avery had also figured it out.

"It's on another path on the other side of those trees," she said.

"Can it get here from there?" Cecilia asked.

"I don't know," Avery said. "This maze is really tricky. I don't know how to get to that path."

"Let's hope the lion doesn't know how to get to this path," Evan said.

"The lions know the forest really well," Avery said.

Cecilia said, "Let's get moving. Try to beat the lion back to the castle."

Rocky led the way. Avery was right behind him with the lamp and Evan and Cecilia were on her heels. Evan was just a black silhouette in front of Cecilia's face.

It was hard being last, Cecilia found. The light was up in front and she couldn't see the path at her feet, so she stumbled a lot.

Then the light changed, and Evan's black silhouette

suddenly shimmered into solid form in front of her. She could see the ground too. She realized they were out from under the tree canopy and back in the clearing under the starlight.

Just in time, too, she thought, *because the lion is sounding closer by the second.*

Avery ran over to the door and put her shoulder to it.

"Give me a hand," she called out. "It's stuck."

Evan and Cecilia threw themselves at the door as well, but all of their efforts made no impression at all.

"It's not stuck," Evan said. "It's locked!"

They looked at each other in horror.

"We'll just have to shout and wake someone up so they can let us in," Avery said.

"If you start shouting, that lion is going to hear, and it will know exactly where we are," Evan said, and Cecilia thought he was probably right.

"What's your suggestion, dweeb?" Avery whispered angrily. "It's a castle. It's designed to keep people out. How are we going to get back inside unless someone unlocks the door and lets us in?"

"I don't know," Evan said just as angrily. "I was just pointing out that if you start shouting, we're going to get

torn to shreds by a black lion before anyone will have time to come down and let us in."

"Then you go in front," Avery said. "And while it's busy eating you, we can escape."

"No, you go in front," Evan said. "There's more of you to eat."

"Oh, both of you shut up," Cecilia said. "And listen to me. I have an idea."

"What is it?" Evan asked, looking up at the cliff face hopefully, in case someone should be looking down and see them.

"I was thinking about the story of King Danyon and Baron Mendoza," Cecilia whispered.

"Now is not the time for that," Avery said. "We're about to get eaten by a lion!"

"Now is exactly the time," Cecilia said. "Listen to me."

"What about it?" Avery asked.

"How did King Danyon manage to sneak out, in front of all those soldiers, and set fire to the catapults?" Cecilia asked.

"I've wondered about that too," Evan said.

"There must be a tunnel," Cecilia said.

"A tunnel?" Avery said, frowning. "Where would it come out?"

"In the well!" Evan said, reading Cecilia's mind once again.

Rocky woofed two sharp warning barks.

"The lion is coming," he was saying.

Cecilia heard it too, a faint rustling of leaves on the path through the forest.

"Hurry!" she yelled.

They sprinted to the old decrepit well and peered down. There was just enough starlight to see that the walls of the well were not smooth, but a jumble of different sizes and shapes of rocks.

"What if you're wrong?" Evan asked.

"We'll just hide in the well until the lion goes away," Cecilia said. "Who's going first?"

"I am," Avery said, pushing past her.

Avery clambered through a gap where part of the wall had collapsed and put one foot down inside, feeling for something to stand on.

"It's all pretty old and slippery," she said.

"Move around the well," Cecilia suggested. "Maybe there's some kind of foothold."

Avery worked her right foot around the edge of the well, then shouted desperately, "Nothing!"

"Quick, the rope," Cecilia said.

Avery handed her the rope and she wound one end a couple of times around one of the pillars next to the well. She tied it off in a reef knot, then added a couple more reefs for safety.

Thank you, Jana! Cecilia thought.

They were always tying pieces of string to hold balloons, and Jana had taught her to tie lots of different knots.

Avery grabbed the rope and tugged it a couple of times to test the knot. She put her feet on the edge of the well and slowly lowered herself down, holding the rope and "walking" down the wall.

"There's a ledge down here," her voice swished up from the depths.

"You go," Cecilia urged Evan. He needed no further encouragement. He swung his leg over the well at the same place Avery had, and copied her actions, climbing swiftly down inside the well.

"There's a tunnel! There's a tunnel!" Avery's excited whisper echoed around and around the old well.

Thinking quickly, Cecilia pulled up the rope and tied the lantern onto the end, lowering it back down to Avery. The rope was wet, no doubt from landing in the water far below.

"How about that lion?" she asked Rocky.

"It's coming fast," Rocky said.

Cecilia had worn her jacket, thinking that it would be cold in the forest at night (which it was). She stripped it off and tied it around Rocky's stomach like a sling.

Then she untied the rope and looped it around the pillar before tying it to the jacket. Rocky jumped up onto the wall of the well.

"Grab the rope," she called down the well. "You can lower Rocky down."

"Okay."

The rope tightened around the pillar.

"Okay, ease it out, gently, gently," Cecilia called down, cradling Rocky against her chest and helping him over the edge of the well.

The rope chafed and slipped around the pillar as the makeshift cradle took the strain. Rocky slipped away out of sight.

"Okay, got him," Avery's voice said.

There was a roar from behind her and Cecilia spun around to see the dark shape of the lion, just visible in the starlight, bounding into the clearing.

"Don't untie Rocky," she yelled. "Hang onto the rope on his side."

Without waiting for them to answer, she leaped over the side of the well and grabbed at the rope.

The lion was already on her, lashing out for her with teeth that glowed like daggers in the blackness of its mouth.

The teeth closed on thin air, and Cecilia was falling, desperately grabbing at the rope, trying to stop (or at least slow) her fall.

Her hands got a grip on the rope. Cecilia slipped down a little farther, and then somehow managed to stop her slide.

She swung wildly around the well and crashed into the rocky face with her knee and then her elbow.

Above her she could hear the beast breathing. She saw its paw, gleaming with razor-sharp claws, reaching down into the well and feeling for her.

"Leave me alone!" she shouted up at the animal.

It growled and grunted something, but in the darkness she had no idea what it was saying.

She slid carefully down the rest of the way until her feet touched a rocky ledge. It was slippery and narrow, with barely enough room for the four of them.

Avery and Evan were standing there, hanging grimly

onto the rope, with Rocky still tied to the bottom of it in her now filthy jacket.

In the wall of the well there was a patch of black nothingness that had to be the entrance to the tunnel.

"That was rambunctious!" Evan said, clearly quite exhilarated now that the immediate danger had passed.

"You always use words even when you don't know what they mean," Avery said, untying Rocky.

"No, I use words even when *you* don't know what they mean," Evan said.

Avery was pulling the rope from around the pillar above them as the lion prowled and growled around the well mouth. She coiled it up and slipped it back over her shoulder before picking up the lantern.

Cecilia said, "This explains how King Danyon defeated Baron Mendoza. He must have snuck through this tunnel, then climbed out behind the soldiers, set the big catapults on fire, then escaped back down the well."

"The soldiers wouldn't have expected anyone to sneak up behind them," Evan said, jumping up and down with excitement.

Then he realized he was making too much noise and stopped.

"But where would the tunnel start from? Inside the castle?" Avery asked. "I've lived here my whole life and I've never seen a tunnel."

"There must be a secret entrance," Cecilia said.

"Let's see where this goes," Avery said.

20
THE QUARTERS

THE CEILING OF the tunnel was rock — low and dangerous, especially to delicate things like heads. The floor was uneven with sudden, unexpected ridges and bumps to make you stumble.

And when you straightened up again, the ceiling was waiting for you with another rocky lump aimed right at your skull.

"Ouch!" Evan shouted for the third time.

"Be quiet," Avery hissed.

"Nobody can hear us down here," Evan said.

"Just be quiet anyway, you never know," Avery said.

"You're such a blabbermouth," Evan said.

"Be quiet!"

Cecilia didn't say a word. She was too busy just trying to stay upright and unscarred. Her elbow was raw and red from where she had crashed into the wall of the well and her knee ached.

The tunnel smelled musty and dank, like old, swampy mud, or the classroom at school after soccer practice on a wet day. She walked along in a crouch so she wouldn't bump her head, and imagined that King Danyon must have crawled along here on his hands and knees.

Cecilia had only glimpses of light to help her see. The walls were dark and mysterious in the heart of the tunnel, and she imagined there were faces embedded in the rock. Fingers of rock on the floor reached up to grip her ankles. Crawling insects and wet slimy things oozed out of the walls with pincers and sharp teeth. She tried not to think about these things because they were scaring her, but her mind wouldn't listen.

This tunnel was old. Very old. The castle and the tunnel had already been here, long deserted, when King Danyon had found it. So the people who built it, digging the tunnel out of solid bedrock, had lived many hundreds, maybe even thousands, of years before Danyon. Who knew what dark magic they practiced or what ancient secrets were buried here?

Rocky padded along quietly behind her, his four feet making easy work of the uneven floor. His presence made

Cecilia a little happier because she knew he would defend her if any ancient spirits came seeping out of the walls.

"What did you see in the tree?" Evan asked. "You were reaching up for something when you fell."

Cecilia reached into the pocket of her jacket and brought out a scrap of material. After she fell from the tree, she had tucked it into her pocket. "This," she said.

Avery, who was leading with the lantern, stopped and turned back for a moment, and they studied the scrap in the weak light.

"It's blue," Evan said.

"It's hard to tell in this light," Cecilia said.

"It's definitely blue," Avery said. "It's from one of the uniforms of the royal guards. How could that have gotten in the tree?"

"They must have gone to look for the balloon after all," Avery said. "Even though the King said not to."

Cecilia had something altogether more sinister rolling around in her mind, but was hesitant to say it.

Rocky looked at her and growled. Cecilia nodded. It was hard to believe, but it had to be true.

"I don't think the balloon floated away on its own," she said, in quiet words that seemed to disappear the moment they were uttered. "I think one of the guards did it."

"That's nuts," Avery said.

"Why?" Evan asked.

"I don't know," Cecilia admitted. "Why would one of the guards not want us to be rescued?"

"The guards just do what the King tells them to do," Avery scoffed.

"Then why would the King not want us to be rescued?" Cecilia asked.

"I don't know," Evan said. Avery shook her head.

"Maybe he likes being a king," Rocky woofed, but Cecilia didn't translate that for the twins.

The tunnel began to slope upward, and every now and then they came to a set of stairs, usually at a right angle to the tunnel. The passage would head off in another direction, then come to more stairs, zigging and zagging its way under the mountain.

They were climbing rapidly now, rising up inside the cliff face. One more flight of stairs and they came to a dead end.

A small wooden door faced them, hardly bigger than a trapdoor in the wall.

Avery wiped her hand across the frame of the door and dislodged a pile of thick gray dust. "Nobody has been here in a very long time," she said.

"So King Harry doesn't know about this tunnel," Evan said.

"Seems that way," Cecilia agreed.

"Everybody be really quiet — especially you, Evan," Avery said. "We don't know where this is going to open into. It could be anywhere."

***

It wasn't anywhere. It was somewhere. Somewhere very special. It was a dining room — a grand dining room with a long table stretching down the center of it.

The table was covered with dust and cobwebs, and clearly hadn't been used for years. All along it, there were chairs . . . although only the wooden frames remained, the fabric coverings having rotted away long ago.

Paintings and canvases that had somehow survived the centuries hung in gold and silver frames on the walls. And the pictures, although slightly faded and covered in dust, were still clear. They were portraits of kings and queens, of princes and princesses.

"We're in the royal quarters," Avery whispered, mesmerized.

She pushed the trapdoor closed behind them and gasped.

They all turned to look.

Here inside the dining room, the entrance to the tunnel was concealed by another painting, one of two that held the place at the head of the table. One of a man, one of a woman. There was no doubt in anybody's mind. This had to be King Danyon and Queen Natassia.

The age, the dust, and the lantern light did them no justice at all, but even so, they took Cecilia's breath away. King Danyon was a handsome man, with a short goatee beard. His hair was long and braided and he wore a crown that Cecilia recognized. She had seen King Harry wearing it just a day before.

Queen Natassia was quite simply beautiful. She wore a crown that matched the King's, although hers held red gems, while King Danyon's sparkled with jewels of blue and green.

"Holy macaroni," Evan said. "It's them!"

"And if that's the King and Queen," Cecilia said, her gaze drifting around the wall to the first portrait on the long side wall. "Then that must be Princess Annachanel."

The Princess looked like her mother. Younger, of course, but she had the same high cheekbones and delicate chin.

"She's wearing the crown," Avery noted.

So this was not Princess Annachanel, Cecilia realized. It was Queen Annachanel. Then the next portrait must be Queen Annachanel's husband — a handsome young man wearing the King's crown. The new King.

On it went, down the wall. Each pair of paintings, a beautiful couple wearing the royal crowns. This was the royal dynasty that had started with Danyon and Natassia and disappeared somewhere in the mists of time.

"Listen," Rocky woofed. Cecilia took her eyes off of the portraits. The noise. It didn't sound like a river now, and it definitely wasn't a ghost.

"Can you hear that?" she asked.

"Come on," Avery said. She led the way down past the ornate dining table to a set of double doors at the far end of the room.

She stopped at the doors and listened.

Rocky sniffed at them and shook his head to say that nobody was outside.

Avery eased open one of the doors and the others followed her out.

They entered a corridor, where the noise was even louder.

"Quietly," Avery whispered.

They crept along the darkened corridor, trying not

to breathe too loudly. The noise grew louder. Ahead of them, a thin line of light glowed from under another set of double doors.

More doors were to the left and right of them. Above each door were signs. They were written in strange old characters, but they were still recognizable words: sitting room, living room, kitchen, parlor, nursery.

The last door on their right, before the double doors at the end, had no sign. But it was here that the whirring, buzzing, humming noise was the loudest.

Avery looked back at the others and raised an eyebrow. Evan and Cecilia both nodded (so did Rocky, but Avery didn't see that).

Avery reached down and grasped the old brass handle of the door securely, then pushed it open.

The noise hit them immediately. It was much louder now: a chugging, throbbing sound that enveloped them.

The door opened into darkness and Avery held up the lantern so they could see into the room.

"What on Earth is that?" Avery asked.

"I don't believe it," Cecilia said.

21
A Shock

CECILIA KNEW WHAT it was immediately, because there was one in her house.

It was a small engine, surrounded by a tubular stainless steel frame. On top of the frame was a red metal cover, while underneath were lots of bits and pieces that she didn't quite understand.

But she knew what it was called and what it did.

It was called a gasoline generator.

It was kind of like a car engine, but it didn't make anything move. Instead it made electricity.

A thick black cable snaked out of the machine and disappeared into a hole high in one of the walls. She told the others what it was and what it did.

But why does the King need electricity? Cecilia wondered.

She could tell that Avery and Evan were having trouble

understanding the very idea of electricity. She realized that they had never in their lives seen an electric light, or a TV set, or any of the other wonderful inventions that electricity made possible.

"Quick," she said. "Shut the door before they notice the sound has gotten louder."

Avery pulled the door shut and they crept farther along the corridor, toward large double doors.

These doors also had no sign, but they didn't need one. Cecilia was sure this would be the royal chamber — the King and Queen's bedroom.

There was sudden laughter from inside the room, and another low background noise that she couldn't identify.

Rocky sniffed at the door, but said nothing.

Light poured through a keyhole at about her waist height. Cecilia sank to her knees and put her eye up to it.

"No way," she whispered. Her legs felt like jelly and her eye slipped from the hole.

"What is it?" Evan whispered.

"Shhh," Avery said.

Cecilia put her eye back to the keyhole. Now she could see why the King needed electricity. Now she knew the truth about King Harry.

Over by a wall a refrigerator sat next to a table. On

the refrigerator was a microwave oven and thin cardboard boxes were stacked in a corner.

Harold the Merciful, King of Storm and all its Environs, was sitting on a sofa with his back to her. Sitting with him on the sofa was Sergeant Lee, the big grizzly bear guard. The other guards were sitting in armchairs scattered around the room.

None of them were looking her way. Their eyes were all glued to a corner of the room. To a glowing screen. A television set!

They were watching an old TV show that Cecilia recognized, a comedy about a bunch of people who are trapped on a desert island.

The King had a television set, a microwave, and a refrigerator, while his subjects lived the life of peasants, working their fingers to the bone in the fields and the mills!

But what shocked her even more was what was in King Harry's hands.

In one hand he held a bottle of beer and, as she watched, he slurped merrily from it.

In his other hand he held a slice of pizza.

22
A New Plan

It is a sad but true fact that there are always some people in the world who think they are better than the rest of us.

Clearly King Harry was one of those people. He thought that he was better than Cecilia and Evan and Avery. He thought he was better than Mrs. Proctor and her beautiful daughter, Jazz, better than Tony Baloney and old Gimpy, and the two plumbers and the three astronomers, and all the other subjects in his kingdom.

Better, even, than you and me.

Some people might say, *Of course he is better than the rest of us — he's the King.*

And why shouldn't a king have nice cold beer, stored in a nice cold refrigerator?

And why shouldn't a king have nice hot pizza, and a

television set to while away all those long evenings when he was not engaged in kingly duties?

Anyone could see that being a king, with all that responsibility and decision making, could be a very difficult and tiring job. As Evan might say: a very fugacious job (although that would be entirely the wrong word to use).

Cecilia was more than a little annoyed that the King had beer and pizza and who knows what other luxuries hidden inside that refrigerator.

But what really got her steamed up were three questions, which probably all had the same answer.

Where did the King get the beer?

Where did he get the gasoline for the generator?

Where did he get the pizza?

***

Evan and Avery shrugged in unison and looked blankly at Cecilia. They were seated in the lower courtyard by the waterfall. Cecilia stopped talking and tried to catch her breath. She had been jabbering at the twins for an hour.

The problem was that they didn't understand most of what she was trying to tell them.

She had spent almost half an hour just trying to explain

what pizza was, how it came from Italy, and how you called up the pizza place, and then the pizza was delivered it in a little red car.

"All the way from Italy?" Avery had asked.

Everything Cecilia tried to explain just led to more questions.

"What's electricity again?" Avery asked at one point, despite the fact that Cecilia had already explained that one three times.

"Okay, okay," Cecilia said finally, drawing in a deep breath. "It comes down to this," she continued. "Those things that King Harry and his goons have hidden in the royal chamber —" she paused and looked around the courtyard, making sure nobody else was around "— they could only have come from outside the forest."

There was silence, except for the rushing water of the waterfall and the bubbling of the birdbath.

"You mean King Harry knows a way out?" Avery said slowly.

"Of course that's what she means, dumbo," Evan said. "Don't be so effervescent."

Cecilia nodded her head. "And back in again. He probably sends his goons out to pick up supplies."

"They can leave any time they want?" Avery was still

struggling to get her head around it, and Cecilia didn't blame her.

After a whole life spent trapped inside the forest, believing that there was no chance of escape, to find out that the King and his zoo just casually came and went as they pleased must have been a little too much to comprehend, really.

"And they ordered pizza and a man came in a little red car and delivered it?" Evan was puzzled by that one.

"Of course he didn't just call and order it," Cecilia said. "I'm almost certain that they don't deliver to ancient castles in black forests. King Harry most likely had it delivered to a house near the forest, and they went and picked it up from there."

"But how?" Avery almost wailed.

"They must know a way through the maze," Evan said. "A shortcut. A path that even the lions don't know."

"And why hasn't he told everybody else?" Avery cried, but quietly, conscious of the dark windows of the castle above them. "Why make the rest of us think there's no way out?"

Rocky lifted his head and looked at Cecilia. He didn't say anything, but she knew what he was thinking.

Smart dog that he was, Rocky had figured it out before anyone.

"Because King Harry likes being a king," Cecilia said. "Here he's royalty, ordering everybody around, and commanding us to do stuff. Like kiss his hand."

"Yuck," woofed Rocky, and Cecilia tried not to laugh.

Even a dog didn't want to kiss that royal hand!

"But out in the real world he'd be nothing," she continued. "A nobody."

"What about his guards?" Evan asked, and then tried out the word that Cecilia had used. "His goons."

"He must pay them somehow," Cecilia decided. "And not just with pizza and beer. Maybe he has a supply of gold or something."

She gritted her teeth and growled angrily, sounding surprisingly like a black lion.

"Who should we tell first?" she asked. "How about your parents? Or Mrs. Proctor? We can call a town meeting, or whatever you do here, and let everybody else know."

The twins were looking at each other. They didn't appear happy.

"How about at dinner?" Cecilia suggested. "Everybody is together then."

"Matthew Skelly," Evan said, shaking his head.

Cecilia raised both eyebrows. "Who is he?"

"Who *was* he," Avery said.

Cecilia just looked at them.

"He was a boy. I think he was about twelve when he disappeared," Evan said.

"He broke into the royal quarters, for a dare," Avery said. "When he came back, he was white as a ghost and wouldn't talk to anyone about anything."

"They must have caught him and threatened him," Cecilia said.

"Two days later he disappeared," Evan said. "Nobody worried too much. People sometimes just disappear around here."

"They are usually trying to find a way out through the maze," Avery said. "Whether they make it or not, nobody knows."

Cecilia thought again of the lions and shuddered.

"But maybe Matthew didn't go into the maze on his own free will," Evan said.

Cecilia was horrified. "You mean they took him into the forest and left him for the lions?"

"Nobody knows," Avery said again. "But everyone thought that the King was teaching him a lesson."

"Well, we have to tell someone," Cecilia said, her voice even softer than before, and her eyes flitting around constantly.

"We'd just be putting them in danger," Evan said.

"Then we'll tell everyone, at dinner, like I said," Cecilia said.

"King Harry will just deny it," Evan said. "And the goons will back him up. And a few days later we'll all disappear."

"Oh," Cecilia said, not liking the sound of that at all. "So what can we do?"

"I don't think there's anything we can do," Avery said. Evan shook his head sadly.

"Of course there is," Cecilia said, lifting her chin and straightening her shoulders. "All we need is a plan."

23
TONY BALONEY

THE NEXT DAY was not a good day for Tony Baloney.

Every day Tony would leave the castle through the stone door and check on his tar traps in the tarblood trees around the clearing.

A tar trap is a small tube painstakingly drilled into a tarblood tree. It took three or four days of drilling to make a hole in the tough bark of the trees, even for a big strong man like Tony Baloney. Then he would insert a tar tube, and a sluggish flow of precious tar, the sap of the tree, would drip through the tube.

Each tube would run for only a week, sometimes less, before the tree would somehow heal itself and the tar would stop flowing. So Tony had a full-time job (except during harvest) drilling, checking the traps, and collecting the tar in a big wooden bucket.

Being a tar man was not a popular job because it involved going out into the clearing, where there was always the danger of lions.

Tony never seemed to mind it though. Some people said that the lions were scared of him, and not the other way around. There was a story that when Tony had first gotten lost in the forest, he had been attacked by a lion and Tony had won. But nobody knew if that was true, and Tony certainly wasn't telling.

"Boomphah!" he would shout as he strode into the clearing. "Boomphah!"

Maybe the strange sound scared away the lions, or maybe they were afraid because they knew who was making the noise.

Either way, Tony had never been attacked while working on the tar traps.

Each night when he returned with his bucket full of tar, it was his responsibility to make sure that the big wooden door braces were replaced, locking the front door to the castle.

The previous day he had helped with the harvest, then went out to check on the traps.

Private Weasel had been doing his rounds just before lights out and had found the big stone door still unlocked.

Tony insisted that when he had returned, he had locked the front door as usual. He kept saying this over and over, miming the action of closing the big stone and putting back the braces. But the guards did not believe him.

"Nobody else would go out there," Sergeant Lee said.

"Big dumb oaf," Private Weasel said.

Tony was sitting on the naughty chair. At least that's how Cecilia thought of it — they had one at school, where children who misbehaved had to sit until they could control their behavior. This chair was a large wooden one from the old days of the castle, and sat in a corner of the throne room.

When the King wanted to interrogate or humiliate someone, he called for a Royal Court of Inquiry. The offending person was forced to sit on the naughty chair, in front of all the other citizens, while Sergeant Lee questioned the person.

The King sat on his throne, watching from a distance, as if detached from the proceedings, but Cecilia saw his beady eyes glinting as he took in every detail.

Tony looked genuinely scared of Sergeant Lee, which Cecilia thought was a little odd. Sergeant Lee might have been large, hairy, and grizzly-bearish in appearance, but Tony was even bigger.

He looked like he could reach out and squeeze Sergeant Lee to a pulp. Yet he cowered, embarrassed, in the chair, protesting his innocence with his mimed movements, but knowing that nobody believed him.

Nobody except Cecilia, Avery, and Evan.

"We have to say something," Cecilia whispered to Avery and Evan as they watched Sergeant Lee bully Tony some more.

"It wasn't him who did it — it was us," she continued. "We can't let him be punished for something that we did."

Avery shook her head. "He'll survive."

Evan agreed. "But if we own up to going out in the forest after dark, they'll start asking lots of other questions and the next thing . . ."

"Matthew Skelly," Avery said.

"No," Cecilia said. "It's just wrong."

Tony's punishment was no dinner.

That was always the punishment, according to Avery, and in a world where there was only just enough to eat at the best of times, to go without dinner was especially cruel.

But not cruel enough for King Harry.

Not only did the offender have to miss out on dinner, he also had to sit on a chair in the banquet hall and watch everybody else eat! Meanwhile, Tony's stomach would probably be rumbling like a steam locomotive. Tonight's meal was a special treat, as well: wild pork chops and honey roasted potatoes.

"How about we each save him half of our dinner?" Evan suggested. "Three half kids' meals would be almost as much as a full grown-up's meal. We can sneak it out and give it to him later."

"Won't he wonder why?" Cecilia asked.

"We'll just tell him we felt sorry for him," Evan said.

"It's still not right," Cecilia said, but she didn't argue anymore.

Especially with the thought of being thrown into the middle of the mazelike, lion-infested forest by Sergeant Lee and the rest of the zoo.

***

After dinner, Cecilia and the twins went down to the cottage where Tony lived. His cottage was on the other side of the river from the castle, so they had to cross over the old stone bridge just down from the courtyard. It was quite secluded, screened from the castle by a stand of maple trees.

They saw him through the window, sitting at his

kitchen table with his head in his hands. Cecilia waved to get his attention. He held up a finger, letting them know he was coming.

It took him a few minutes to answer, and when he did, it was clear from his red, smeary eyes that he had been crying. Cecilia had never seen a grown man cry before, and felt a little embarrassed.

Tony managed a half-smile and lifted a hand to say hello.

Cecilia and the twins had snuck their meals out of the dining room by wrapping them in a cloth and concealing them in Cecilia's jacket, which she carried casually in one hand.

She unwrapped the food and held it up.

Big Tony Baloney looked as though he was going to start crying again, but he shook his head.

"Yes," Cecilia said, and the others nodded in agreement. "This is for you."

Tony looked at the food for a long moment, then looked at them, and finally took the meal, and put it down on a table inside his cottage. Then he returned to the doorway.

He tapped his chest with three fingers and said quietly, "Boomphah."

Cecilia instinctively reached out and took his hand. She tapped her own chest with her free hand and repeated, "Boomphah."

Tony smiled hugely, but then his expression changed. As he had been doing in the throne room, he mimed the action of putting back the braces on the big stone door.

I did put them back! he was saying.

Cecilia looked at the others. They shook their heads.

"We have to," Cecilia said. "It wouldn't be honest not to." She took a deep breath, unsure of the reaction she was going to get. She pointed to herself, then to Evan and Avery, and mimed the action of taking down the braces.

We know you didn't. It was us.

There was a drawing in of breath from the giant, and the twins drew back a little from the doorway. Then Tony relaxed and even smiled.

He put one huge hand over his mouth and winked at them.

I won't tell anyone!

24
Nothing Happened

HARVEST WEEK WAS a week of hard work, finishing with the big Harvest Festival party on Saturday night.

Everybody was busy picking, cutting, packing, hauling, and storing the various crops that kept the community fed throughout the year.

On Wednesday, Summer Busch, who lived in the first cottage over the bridge with her husband, Wilfred, had a baby, which made a total of three children who had been born in Storm in modern times. (The other two, of course, were Avery and Evan.)

On Thursday everybody was summoned to the throne room before dinner for another Royal Court of Inquiry.

Much to Cecilia's horror, Summer was sitting in the naughty chair that night, clutching her newborn baby in her arms.

King Harry was outraged. It wasn't the baby that made him so angry. It was the fact that the baby had been born during harvest week.

The King sat on his throne at the end of the room and fumed (Cecilia could almost see the steam coming out of his ears) as the big sergeant scolded Summer for being so lazy.

"Any excuse to get out of helping with the harvest," Sergeant Lee thundered.

"But the baby came early!" Wilfred Busch cried out from the back of the room, trying to stand up for his wife. "It wasn't our fault."

"Well, it certainly wasn't my fault," Sergeant Lee yelled, going a little red in the face. "Whose fault was it?"

Wilfred seemed to shrink down inside himself, deflating like a balloon with a leak.

"Well?" Lee demanded.

"It wasn't anybody's fault," Summer said. "She just came early. Look. She's beautiful."

Lee didn't seem to hear her. "Or was it perhaps King Harold's fault?"

"No, sir, of course not," Summer said, clutching the baby closer as if he was going to take her away.

Big Tony Baloney was standing next to Cecilia. He

shuddered every time Sergeant Lee shouted. Cecilia reached up and took his hand. He looked down at her and his eyes were sad.

"It's not fair," Cecilia whispered.

Although he could not hear her, Tony must have understood what she meant, because he shook his head.

Sergeant Lee looked over at the King. Cecilia saw the King discreetly raise two fingers off the arm of the throne.

"You are sentenced to two nights without dinner," Sergeant Lee said.

There was a gasp from the crowd.

Two nights. That was a very severe punishment.

Summer lowered her eyes and held her baby close.

"You can't do that," Cecilia said loudly before she knew what she was doing.

All eyes turned to her. Sergeant Lee stiffened, drawing himself up to his full height and turning in her direction. The King was furious, Cecilia saw, but it was too late to turn back.

"You can't," she said. "She has a new baby. The baby needs food, and she gets that from her mother. If you starve Mrs. Busch, you are starving the baby too."

Sergeant Lee started to march in Cecilia's direction, but stopped as a bulky shape moved slightly in front of her.

Big Tony Baloney let go of her hand and took a step forward. To get to her, Sergeant Lee would have to go around him.

The other guards were on their feet now, drawing wooden batons from their belts and looking at the King for instructions.

"She's right!" yelled Wilfred. "It's a cruel and unusual punishment."

Cecilia thought that Harold the Merciful was a cruel and unusual king.

By now the crowd was starting to stir with a deep undercurrent of discontent.

The King, clearly uncomfortable, stayed silent for a moment, while the guards, with their batons drawn, waited for instructions.

The mood of the crowd darkened and the tension swelled, like a big, festering pimple that was just waiting to burst.

"I will be merciful," King Harry said at last, attempting to sound calm and compassionate, but his anger was spitting out with every word. "I hereby pardon Mrs. Summer Busch for her crime, and transfer the punishment to Ms. Cecilia Undergarment."

***

Cecilia did not go hungry.

That night, as she wandered back to her quarters, there was a quick rustle of clothing and a bump against her arm, and when she looked down there was a package in her hand that hadn't been there before.

She turned to look, but saw only a flash of gray tunic as the person disappeared around a corner.

The package turned out to be a loaf of cheese bread, wrapped in catichoke leaves. And that was just the start.

Almost every person she passed — even people she hadn't met yet — shook her hand, and when they let go she would be holding a scrap of food.

And when she went back to her room there were fruits and breads, carefully wrapped and hidden under her mattress.

Like it or not, Cecilia had become a small hero in the gorge. She certainly hadn't intended to be, or planned it that way, but it was sort of a nice feeling anyway.

But in another way it was a little disturbing.

She had the sense that many people in the valley were not quite happy with the way things were run by the King and his henchmen. For years they had put up with it, uncomplaining, accepting their situation.

Somehow Cecilia's arrival and her taking a stand

against the King had changed all that. She caught the edges of muttered conversations where the King's name was often mentioned, and the expressions on peoples' faces were grim.

The King seemed to be aware of this, and that night his guards strode through the castle, eavesdropping on conversations or breaking up groups of people who had gathered to chat.

On Friday morning she passed the King at the main entrance to the castle, but he did not speak to her. He shot her a narrowed glance, and his nostrils flared, before he stomped back up the stairs to the royal quarters.

He didn't like her much, she decided, but that was okay. The feeling was mutual.

***

That afternoon, Cecilia and the twins went swimming.

Cecilia had finished helping Jazz grind the flour by around three o'clock and was playing fetch with Rocky, using a short stick she'd snapped off a fallen oak branch.

They had only been playing for about twenty minutes when Avery and Evan appeared along the riverbank.

"What happened?" she asked. "Shouldn't you still be harvesting?"

Evan grinned. "Finished."

"We picked the entire crop of crawling beans," Avery said. "Tomorrow they'll put us on a different crew, but for the rest of the day we're free."

"We're going for a swim," Evan said. "You want to come? It'll be salubrious."

Avery rolled her eyes, and Cecilia laughed.

"But I don't have a swimsuit," Cecilia said.

"What's a swimsuit?" Evan asked.

Cecilia looked at him carefully to be sure he wasn't making fun of her.

"It's like a special costume you wear when you go swimming," she said. "Otherwise you'd be completely naked."

Avery and Evan looked one another in the eyes and laughed.

"You wear clothes when you go swimming?" Avery asked.

"Don't they get wet?" Evan asked.

"Well, they're special swimming clothes," Cecilia said. "They're supposed to get wet."

Avery and Evan laughed again.

"That's funny," Avery said.

"No it's not," Cecilia said.

"We don't wear special swimming clothes," Evan said. "Around here, nobody minds."

"It's what everybody does," Avery said.

"I think I'll leave my undies on," Cecilia said, crossing her arms and lifting her chin determinedly into the air.

"What are undies?" Evan asked.

It was a long way to the waterhole, which was right at the far end of the gorge.

On the way they passed Tony and his harvest gang. They were working at one of the widest parts of the gorge, where the steep rocky walls sloped inward on both sides, creating a terrifying overhang.

The top of the gorge was still narrow here, but at the base, it had been worn away by the river to create a wide plain. Small beech forests grew on both banks of the river.

As they passed, Tony banged his chest a couple of times. "Boomphah! Boomphah!"

Cecilia and the twins waved from the other side of the river.

Tony had an animal on a leash. At first Cecilia thought it was a dog, but then she realized it was a pig.

"I didn't know Tony had a pet pig," she said.

Then, as Cecilia watched the harvest gang wander in and out of beech trees, she noticed that all the harvesters had pigs of their own, all on leashes. All of the pigs were wearing muzzles.

"They're truffling," Evan said. "That's one of our biggest crops."

Cecilia thought of all the large sacks that Tony and his gang had been hauling back from the river earlier that week.

"What's a truffle?" she asked.

Avery said, "They're these big white things kind of like mushrooms."

"They grow underground, and the pigs help find them," Evan said. "But they're nothing like mushrooms."

"Yes they are," said Avery.

"Not at all," said Evan.

"They're both funguses," Avery said.

"Fungi," Evan said.

Cecilia wanted to ask more about the truffles, but she couldn't get a word in edgewise.

Then they reached the waterhole and she completely forgot about it.

Here at the far end of the gorge, the river tumbled whitely over rapids, splashing over rocks, spitting long streams of foam into the air, and bubbling down into a wide rock pool that narrowed again at one end, where huge jagged boulders seemed to have fallen from the cliff above.

The water surged through a gap in the boulders before vanishing into a crevice in the cliff face.

"Is it safe?" Cecilia asked.

"Who cares?" Avery grinned.

Evan nodded. "It's very safe as long as you stay away from the rapids and the outlet." He pointed to the hole in the cliff where the water surged and frothed before disappearing underground.

The bank on this side of the river sloped gradually into the swimming hole.

Evan and Avery threw off their clothes and raced each other down the slope, disappearing abruptly into the water.

Their heads popped back up, laughing.

"Come on," they both yelled.

"Turn around!" Cecilia shouted back.

They did (eventually) and Cecilia got undressed behind a bush, before she ran down the ramp and jumped into the water behind them.

They played and splashed around for half an hour, refreshed by the cool, clear water.

Once or twice Cecilia found herself heading in the

direction of the outlet and felt cold, watery hands grasp at her, pulling her toward the jagged rocks.

She was careful to stay far away from it.

***

It was on the way back that she told them about her new plan.

"Tomorrow night, when everybody is at the Harvest Festival dance, we should sneak back into the royal chambers," she said.

"During the dance!" Evan was horrified.

"The dance is the perfect time," Cecilia explained earnestly. "Everyone else will be busy, so we can have a good look around without having to worry about being discovered."

"But we wait all year long for the Festival!" Evan said. "It's the highlight of the year. The one day we all look forward to."

"It's just a stupid dance," Avery said.

"Listen," Cecilia said. "If there really is a way out of Northwood, don't you want to know about it?"

"Of course," Avery said, with a nervous flicker of her eyes.

Evan hesitated before nodding, and Cecilia realized that neither of the twins had ever seen the outside world. They had been born in the castle, and the thought of the world outside must be very scary for them.

Once they got out, she would do all she could to help them to adjust. She would teach them about her world, as they had been teaching her about theirs.

"If there is a path through the forest that nobody knows about," Cecilia said, "then there must be a map. Otherwise, how would King Harry know about it? You can bet he wasn't smart enough to find it by himself."

"He's not smart enough to find his own nose by himself," Evan said.

"So we break into the royal chambers during the dance and find the map," Cecilia said. "Then we can lead everybody out into the world, and expose King Harry for the liar, cheat, and thief that he really is."

The twins agreed, although still with a little bit of hesitation.

"We don't all need to go down the well," Cecilia said. "Only one of us does. Then that person can open the door to the royal chambers and let the others in."

"I'll go," Avery said immediately.

"No, it has to be me," Cecilia said. "I'm not strong enough to help put the braces back on the door. And we can't get poor Tony in trouble again."

They all agreed on that.

25
THE PARTY

EVERYONE WORE THEIR best clothes to the Harvest Festival dance.

For most, that was the same gray smocks they wore during the day, but they decorated them brightly with flowers, sashes, and colored ribbons so that the courtyard looked like a kaleidoscope of whirling, twirling shapes.

Avery's mother had helped Cecilia by tying some scraps of material into bows and pinning them onto her shoulders.

When Cecilia asked where the colored material came from, Mrs. Celestine told her they were the few remaining scraps of the dress she had been wearing when she had gotten lost in the forest. Most people had some remnants of their "world" clothes, and some even had the entire outfit, bringing it out only at festival time.

The round, raised area that Cecilia had seen earlier was indeed a band rotunda, although Castle Storm didn't actually have much of a band.

The royal orchestra had only one real instrument in it: a banjo that old Gimpy had been carrying when he had wandered into Northwood.

But they had created other instruments out of things around them. A set of drums made by stretching some kind of thin leather over a frame made from branches. A wooden board with ridges that was used for washing clothes became a rhythm instrument played by Mrs. Clarkevy. And Mr. Knight, the oldest person in Storm, had a box with a long pole on the top. He plucked at a string stretched between the top of the pole and the box, producing a low bass note.

The music was brimming with energy, as if by playing and singing and dancing, the people of Storm could lift themselves out of their dreary world to a colorful place, even if only for an hour or so.

The courtyard was lit with flaming torches, casting flickering light across the revelers' faces. The little golden statue of the bird in the waterfall had been polished and shone like a beacon.

At exactly nine o'clock, the music suddenly stopped,

and everybody retreated to the low wall around the courtyard, finding seats where they could.

Old Gimpy put down his banjo and picked up his "trumpet," the wooden horn that he had used in the throne room.

A long, clear note sounded, then a short salute, and the King, in fine velvet robes, appeared. He sat on a carriage, carried on poles on the shoulders of four of the strongest men in the gorge, one of whom was big Tony Baloney.

Four men of the royal guard, in their bright-blue finery, walked behind the carriage. The men set the carriage at the head of the courtyard and the King clapped his hands twice.

"I now declare the festival open," he said grandly.

The music started again immediately, and people poured back into the center of the courtyard to dance.

***

Cecilia, Avery, and Evan waited until the party was in full swing before sneaking into the castle one by one and making their way down to the big stone door.

They pushed the door open slightly. Rocky stuck his nose out and sniffed a few times, then winked at Cecilia.

"No lions," she whispered to the others. She pushed

the door open a little wider and slipped through before she lost her nerve.

The sound of the big stone door closing behind her sent a shudder through her heart.

No lions, Rocky had told her. But that didn't mean there weren't any prowling the pathways nearby. The well looked a long way off.

She took a step, then another, and before she knew it she was almost halfway to the well — halfway from the safety of the castle.

She glanced back, realizing that there was no safety there. The big door was shut. If a lion came into the clearing now, it would be on her before the twins could open the door and pull her inside. Her only chance was to get to the well.

Without making a noise, she quickened her pace, trotting as fast as she dared through the grass of the clearing, which was lit only by the moon.

She had a lantern with her, but had not lit it. It would be too easy for the light to be seen from the castle, and she didn't want to risk it.

The faint moonlight was just enough for her to make her way to the well without tripping over anything or getting lost in the darkness.

She took her coil of rope and tied it securely around her waist before looping it twice around a stone pillar.

Holding it firmly, Cecilia clambered over the edge of the well, half expecting to hear rushing footsteps and the gnashing teeth of a lion at any moment.

She let out the rope slowly and walked backward down the vertical face of the well. She only felt safe when she was low enough to be out of a lion's reach.

Once she got to the ledge, she pulled the rest of the rope down into the well after her, leaving no trace of her expedition visible from above.

A few minutes later, she had completed part one of the mission.

She opened the doors to let the twins and Rocky into the royal quarters.

The carefree beat of Latin music bounced its way to them along the corridors and stairways of the castle like a small boy bouncing a ball against a fence. But the melody and the singing were swallowed up by the rock or drowned out by the constant whir of the gasoline generator at the other end of the hall.

"One of us needs to stand guard," Evan said, "in case King Harry or any of his zoo leave the party early or decide to check on something."

"Rocky will do that," Cecilia said. "He'll bark if he hears or smells anyone approaching. Won't you, Rocky?" She added, "Good boy," which earned her a disdainful look from the Samoyed.

"If anybody comes, we all go to the dining room and hide in the tunnel," Evan said.

Avery nodded. "Let's see if we can find this map."

"I'll take the nursery," Cecilia said.

"I'll take the sitting room," said Evan.

"Okay. I'll take the drawing room," Avery said.

***

It must have been a nursery once, because that was what it said over the door, but the room Cecilia was searching through had clearly most recently been used as the bedroom of a little girl.

A princess! This was Princess Annachanel's bedroom, then her children's, and then her children's children's.

The last little girl who had lived in this room would have been the daughter or granddaughter of Queen Annachanel, Cecilia thought, *before all the people in the castle mysteriously disappeared.*

They must have left in a hurry. The dining room was filled with furniture and paintings, and here in the princess's bedroom there was still a four-poster bed and a freestanding closet, although it had sagged with age and was now leaning against one wall.

The bed was even made with ragged old blankets that might have once been pink, although moths and rot had long since eaten away at them. A chest of drawers still stood proudly against one wall, a mirror above it in a wooden frame. The mirror was cracked in two directions and covered with dust.

Cecilia wiped the glass with her hand, carefully avoiding the cracks, and looked at herself standing in the bedroom of a real princess.

Her heart began to beat faster. A princess had stood exactly where she was standing now, as maids brushed her hair and fussed over her gown, preparing her for a banquet or a royal ball. What must it have been like?

She opened the closet, wondering if any of the princess's gowns could possibly have survived the centuries, but it was empty.

She bent down and looked under the wardrobe, which was raised on four legs of turned wood. There was just dust and cobwebs.

This room had not been disturbed for centuries, she realized. If there was a map hidden somewhere in the castle, it was not going to be in here. Just to be sure, she peered under the bed.

The frame of the bed had sagged in the center so that the mattress (or what was left of it, at least) was almost resting on the floor. Which is why she didn't see it at first.

She was just about to get back to her feet when she caught a glimpse of something wedged under the collapsed mattress.

Cecilia reached right under the bed, hoping there would be no spiders or cockroaches waiting for her, and she felt something solid. She tugged and it gradually came free from its prison.

Covered in dust and all kinds of grime, it was still easily recognizable. A golden bejeweled tiara.

Cecilia could see it happening.

In their rush to leave the castle the tiara was dropped, or maybe placed on the bed and knocked off. Maybe a careless foot kicked it under the bed and there was no time to search for it.

Whatever had driven these people from the castle must have been sudden and terrifying.

She stood up and blew some of the dust off the tiara. It sparkled in the low light of the lamp.

There was a quiet tap on the door.

Cecilia jumped and turned to see Avery standing there with a strange look on her face.

"You'd better come to the drawing room," Avery said. "You need to see this."

"Look what I found," Cecilia said.

"Nice." Avery sounded as though her find was much more interesting.

"It's a tiara," Cecilia said.

"Bring it with you." Avery was in a hurry.

Cecilia shook her head. "No, it belongs here."

She slid it carefully back under the bed and blew some dust around the floor to hide the scuff marks where she had dragged it out.

It wasn't her tiara — it belonged to a princess. And even if that princess had lived hundreds of years ago, Cecilia didn't feel that the tiara was hers to take.

That wouldn't have been honest.

26
THE DRAWING ROOM

"THIS IS VIVACIOUS!" Evan said.

The drawing room was very long. It seemed more like a corridor than a room and it was not at all what Cecilia was expecting. Each wall of the room was covered with drawings — pictures drawn in simple black ink on square plaques of white marble. Like everything else, they were dusty, but the pictures were perfectly clear.

The drawings were hung in long rows that stretched right down the length of the room.

Cecilia studied the closest ones.

"See, they tell a story," Avery said. "Start with the first picture on the top row and follow them along. Each one is a scene out of a story."

"It's like a comic book," Cecilia said. "Or a graphic novel!"

"What are those?" Evan asked, but Cecilia was too caught up in the panels to answer.

"Here are Baron Mendoza's troops attacking little Prince Danyon's town," she said. "And here are Danyon and Natassia running for their lives."

"Yes, and here they find the castle," Avery said, "and begin to build a new life. And look at all the people who start to arrive at Storm."

That panel showed the new King and Queen standing on the ramparts of the castle watching lines of people streaming in from all directions. Cecilia took her gaze from the panel and looked down the length of the room. "There must be hundreds of pictures here," she said.

"I know," Avery said. "But I wanted to see the part where Danyon burns the catapults, so I skipped all these and just went along till I found it. You're not going to believe it when you see it."

Avery strode past panels showing feasts and celebrations, births and deaths, harvests and droughts.

"Here," Avery said at last.

It was just as Cecilia had seen it in her mind's eye when reading the story. The strong castle standing resolute against the attackers. The huge catapults hurling jagged rocks toward the cliff face. The dark figure of King

Danyon appearing beside the war machines with a burning brand. The tar pits, long trenches concealed in the grass, bursting into flames beneath the catapults. Fire lighting up the cliff face as the weapons were destroyed.

"They don't show the well, though," Cecilia said. "Or the secret passageway."

"Of course not," Evan said. "That was still a secret, even after the battle was won."

Avery said, "See this one? That's the Baron himself wailing in agony as his catapults were destroyed. Here he is again — and again here."

Cecilia looked where Avery was pointing. "Oh my word," she said. There was no doubt. These were drawings of Baron Mendoza. The commander of the army. The archenemy of King Danyon, Queen Natassia, and Castle Storm itself. One panel showed just the Baron's face, agonizing over his defeat. Other panels showed him standing alongside his soldiers.

To Cecilia's shock, she recognized him. Even from a simple line drawing, the man was quite distinctive. He was only around half the height of most of his soldiers. And he was fat, round like a beach ball, with long hair tied back in a ponytail.

"You don't think . . ." Evan's voice trailed off.

"Surely not," Cecilia said.

"It must be," Avery said.

"It's King Harry!" Evan said, and then he said something that his mother would have been very disappointed to hear coming out of his mouth.

"It can't be," Avery said. "This happened hundreds of years ago."

"It's not King Harry," Cecilia agreed. "It's Baron Mendoza. He must be Harry's great-, or great-great-, or great-great-great-grandfather."

"How?" Avery asked. "How did Harry get here?"

Cecilia thought about it for a while. "Maybe Harry knew the story of his great-great-great-grandfather, and came looking for the castle. Somehow he found it, then he set himself up as King. As other people found the place, they became his subjects."

They were all silent for a moment.

It had taken hundreds of years, but Baron Mendoza, or at least his descendant, had finally conquered Castle Storm.

"When everyone finds out that King Harry is a descendant of Baron Mendoza, there's going to be a riot," Avery said. "And this time we've got proof."

"This isn't proof," Evan said.

"He's right," Cecilia said. "Just because King Harry looks like the Baron doesn't mean anything for certain."

"And what about the guards?" Avery asked. "King Harry's little zoo. Why do they do everything he says? Does he pay them with something?"

"Gold, silver?" Cecilia wondered. "Is there a secret treasure room somewhere? The people all seem to have left in a hurry. Maybe they had to leave their treasure behind."

"A treasure room." Avery's eyes lit up. "Full of jewelry and gold! We've got to find it."

"I didn't say there was one," Cecilia said. "I was just wondering."

"What happened to all the people?" Evan asked. "All the descendants of King Danyon and Queen Natassia, and all the other people who came to live in Storm Gorge? Where did they all disappear to in such a hurry?"

"Let's keep reading," Cecilia said. "We might find out."

She was right.

"Here!" Evan said.

He had gone straight to the end of the room, on the right-hand side. The wall on the left was completely covered in drawings, but the right side petered out about halfway down.

"There was an earthquake," Evan said, pointing to a panel. "Part of the cliff collapsed at the far end of the gorge. It dammed up the river where it flows out underground. With the outlet blocked, the river began to rise and rise. It began to fill the gorge, flooding it with water."

Cecilia stared at the next series of drawings in horror. The story was quite clear. All the stone cottages were submerged, and then the water began to rise higher and higher inside the castle itself.

"This is the last panel," Cecilia murmured. "They must have evacuated the gorge and the castle. Moved away. Found somewhere else to live."

It was a shocking end to the story of Storm, Cecilia felt. The mighty castle half flooded: deserted, abandoned, left to rot in the depths of the forest.

"But what happened next?" Avery asked. "How did it get unblocked again?"

"We don't know," Cecilia said. "We can't know. Nobody was here to tell the story."

"Maybe another earthquake jolted the boulders free and unblocked the river," Evan suggested.

Cecilia thought of the large granite boulders surrounding the hole at the end of the rock pool.

"I think that's right," she said.

"Let's keep looking," Avery said. "Maybe the map is hidden somewhere in these drawings."

***

They spent the next ten minutes reading panel after panel from the huge storyboard that lined the walls of the drawing room.

There were hundreds of stories on those walls: births and deaths, tragedies and triumphs. But there were no clues to any secret path that might lead them out of the forest.

"Time to go," Evan said. "Before they notice we're missing."

"Just a minute," Avery said. She had wandered back to the other side of the hall.

"Here's a drawing of Princess Annachanel walking alone in the forest," Avery said.

"No black lions back in those days," Cecilia said.

"I know," Avery said. "Here she is with some birds and squirrels, and . . . what's that? Like a fox or something? Lots of little animals, anyway."

"The forest was probably teeming with animals back in those days," Evan said. "There are probably a lot fewer now, thanks to the lions."

"Yeah," Avery said. "Look at the little lines coming out of the princess's mouth."

Evan didn't seem very interested. He was already opening the drawing room door and checking for sounds in the corridor.

"And the lines coming out of the animals' mouths," Avery said.

Cecilia looked more closely at the panel. Her tongue seemed suddenly dry and she could hear the beating of her heart in her ears. The room seemed to fade into a gray fog around her. There was nothing in the world except her and the drawing.

Avery's voice seemed to be coming from a million miles away as she said, "It's almost like Princess Annachanel is talking to the animals."

27
Naughty Chair

THERE WAS A low growl from the corridor. Cecilia didn't need to see Rocky to understand what he was saying this time.

Danger!

"Come on!" Avery said. "The dining room."

Cecilia tried to move, but her feet were fixed to the floor in front of the picture. She was aware of Evan and Avery running across the corridor and into the dining room, but she could not move her eyes from the little princess talking to the animals of the forest.

"Cecilia," she heard Avery whisper harshly across the hall, and there was a low whine from Rocky.

That, perhaps, was what she needed.

She broke her gaze from the picture and ran to the door of the drawing room.

She took one step out into the hallway and froze. The door to the royal quarters was already starting to open.

Across the hallway she could see Avery's horrified eyes and the urgent waving motion: *Come on!*

But it was too late.

She stepped back inside the drawing room and shut the door quietly as footsteps and voices sounded in the corridor.

She looked desperately around, searching for somewhere to hide. The room was long and straight, with no furniture to crouch behind or alcoves to duck into.

Cecilia flattened herself against the wall by the door. That way if they glanced into the room, they would not see her.

And why would they come into the room anyway? Surely, there was no reason.

The voices in the corridor stopped abruptly.

Her lantern! She was still holding her lantern. Could they see the light underneath the drawing room door?

That question was answered with a crash as the door was flung open. Cecilia grabbed at the knob of the lantern, but it was already far too late.

The glow was like a lighthouse signaling her position as Wolf stormed into the room, his own lantern held high, his other fist clenched. He relaxed slightly when he saw that his foe was just a ten-year-old girl.

Private Weasel came into the room behind him and peered over his shoulder at her.

"Now who do we have here?" Wolf growled.

***

The naughty chair was extremely uncomfortable. There was no way to get comfortable on the uneven surface, which was probably the point.

"How did you get in, you horrible little girl?" Sergeant Lee was thunder and lightning, his face close to hers, flecks of spittle flying in every direction.

Cecilia didn't like being shouted at, and she didn't like being spat on, and she didn't like Sergeant Lee very much either.

The rest of the citizens, still in their party clothes, were gathered at the back of the throne room. None of them looked happy.

"And where are those nasty little friends of yours?" the King said, angrily.

Cecilia glanced at the twins' mom and dad, silently standing at the back of the room with horrified looks on their faces, but she said nothing.

She had never told a lie in her life, but if she told the truth now, they would find the secret passage and Avery and Evan.

She couldn't give them up.

Eventually she said quietly, "I'm not going to say anything."

"Oh yes you are," Lee said in a low, menacing voice.

Cecilia struggled to think.

Her brain wasn't working well with all the shouting and spitting. What was that line they always said in the movies?

"I have the right to remain silent," she said.

That seemed to throw him off course for a moment.

"Did you have a copy of the key?" he asked.

"I have the right to remain silent," Cecilia said again.

"Did you pick the lock?"

"I have the right to remain silent."

"What were you doing in the royal quarters?"

"I have the right to remain silent."

If he'd asked her how to spell rhododendron or what the capital of Iceland was, she would have answered just the same.

King Harry had been sitting quietly watching the proceedings, his face a dark chasm.

Now he yelled out, "She's a spy!"

"How could she be a spy?" Mrs. Proctor called out, quite reasonably, from the back of the room. "She's just a little girl. And anyway, what is there to spy on?"

If only you knew! Cecilia thought.

In her mind she had been debating whether to reveal what they had found out about the King.

They had no way of proving it, but if she told everybody what they had found, then it would be up to the King to prove that he wasn't a descendant of the evil Baron Mendoza.

"She's a thief!" the King cried.

"A nasty little thief," Sergeant Lee agreed.

"And a traitor!" King Harry yelled.

"A treacherous little traitor!"

"As well as a spy!" The King was getting quite carried away now.

"A despicable little spy!"

"I'm not a spy, a thief, or a traitor," Cecilia said. "The truth is that I found a very interesting picture, and I think it shows that King Harry is really —"

That was all she got out before a hand was clamped over her mouth and Sergeant Lee's eyes were just in front of her own, boring into her like two electric drills.

He spoke quietly, so that only she would hear. "People who talk too much around here have a way of disappearing."

Cecilia's words froze in her throat.

"She's a spy," King Harry said again. "To the dungeon with her."

28

Darkness

ALONG WITH SHOUTING and spitting and Sergeant Lee, Cecilia didn't like dungeons much either.

In fact, they were on top of her list of dislikes.

Private Skunk led her down to the dungeons, which she hadn't even known existed. *Why would a good, benevolent king like Danyon need dungeons?* she wondered.

Then she reminded herself that King Danyon hadn't built the castle, he had merely come to live in it. Perhaps whoever had built it, all those years ago, had needed dungeons.

Walking along next to the guard, she found out why the twins called him Skunk. Some people are born smelly. Some people achieve smelliness. Others have smelliness thrust upon them. Cecilia wasn't sure which type of person Private Skunk was, but she suspected all three.

As she walked, she turned her face away from him, hoping that would make a difference.

It didn't.

The dungeons were deep within the castle, on the lowest level, well below the entrance with the big stone door.

The original builders of the castle had not smoothed the walls of these caves, or flattened the floor. They had just built a door of heavy brass bars across the entrance to a cave. The bars, although green and decrepit, still looked strong.

The light from Skunk's lantern briefly let her see inside the dungeon, and it looked horrible. Water seeped down one of the walls, which was mottled purple and green. There was no bed or mattress — just a hard and uneven rock floor.

"You can't put me in there," Cecilia cried out when she saw it, almost gagging on the pungent fumes given off by her prison guard. "That's barbaric!"

"You get what you deserve," Skunk muttered.

There was a heavy brass key hanging on a hook on one of the walls outside the dungeon. He took it, struggling with the ancient brass lock for a moment, before there was a dull click and the door opened.

"Get inside," he said, and shoved her forward at the same time. She sprawled on the harsh, unfriendly rock of the floor. By the time she had gotten back to her feet, the door was shut, and there was another click as it locked.

"You can't leave me here!" she yelled, as Skunk replaced the key on the hook and slunk back up the stairs.

He didn't say anything.

And then there was nothing.

Just darkness.

Complete and utter darkness.

***

You lose track of time when there is nothing to help you measure it by. With no sunlight or moonlight, or even the glow of a lantern, there was no way of knowing whether a minute had passed or an hour.

Even once Cecilia's eyes adjusted to the lack of light, she could not see her own hand if she held it right in front of her face.

It was almost as quiet as it was dark.

Down here there was no sound from the gasoline generator upstairs, no gentle breathing of the wind, no shuffling of feet in the corridors.

Yet there were sounds. She became aware of the air

moving through her nostrils and the quiet beating of her heart.

She listened for the feet of rats, or other tiny creatures, but it seemed that even they didn't like this cave.

There was nothing.

Only her.

Cecilia.

Was that footsteps she could hear in the distance, coming down the stairs?

She felt her way across the floor to the door.

Using the bars for balance, she stood upright and strained her eyes toward where she remembered the stairs were.

Was that the tiniest imagining of a faint glow?

It was!

The light strengthened, and already she could make out the entrance to the stairway.

More — she could see the bars of the door in front of her face.

A lantern appeared at the bottom of the stairway and there were hushed voices.

Voices she recognized.

"Avery! Evan!" she cried out. "Over here!"

"Cecilia." They hurried across to the door.

"There's a key on the wall over there," Cecilia said, pointing.

Evan fetched it, and they struggled with the lock for a few minutes.

Cecilia listened for any more footsteps on the stairs as they worked the lock, but there was nothing. Finally, the lock clicked open.

"Thank you, thank you!" Cecilia cried, hugging them both.

"Hurry, we have to get out of here," Evan said.

"Where to?" Cecilia asked as they headed back up the stairs.

"Tony Baloney's house," Avery said. "They won't think of looking for you there."

"And that will give us time to work out what we're going to do about the King," Evan said.

"What happened to you guys?" Cecilia asked. "After I was caught."

"We hid in the tunnel," Avery said. "They searched all the rooms after they found you, but they still don't know about the secret passage."

Evan added, "We had to wait until the Court of Inquiry, when everybody was gathered in the throne room, before we could slip out."

"What about Rocky?" Cecilia asked.

"He's fine. He's with Mrs. Proctor," Avery said.

They were just coming up to the next level, a creepy cave full of stalactites and stalagmites, with deep alcoves and rocky protrusions.

"Thank you for rescuing me," Cecilia said. "It was horrible in there."

"I didn't expect it to be so easy," Avery said.

Evan stopped dead in his tracks. Since he was the one who was carrying the lantern, Cecilia and Avery stopped with him.

"It *was* easy," he said. "Too easy. What kind of idiot leaves the key to the prison hanging just outside the prison door?"

"Skunk," Cecilia said.

"He's not the tallest tree in the forest," Evan said. "But even he's smart enough to take the key away with him."

"It's a trap!" Cecilia realized with horror.

"They wanted you to escape," Avery said.

"They wanted to catch us too," Evan said. "We've got to get out of here, now!"

Already it was too late.

Four large men stepped out of the shadows and surrounded them.

The men had heavy black sacks, and a moment later Cecilia found herself tied inside one, bouncing along on somebody's shoulder.

"Where are you taking us?" she heard Evan cry.

But Cecilia had a horrible feeling that she already knew.

29
Out of Fear

ALL THE AIR whooshed out of Cecilia's body as the sack she was in hit the ground hard.

There were two more thuds nearby. Evan squealed in pain, and Avery called someone a name that was not very nice.

Then footsteps retreated and they were left alone. Even without seeing, Cecilia knew where they were from the sound of the wind through the trees around them.

They were somewhere in the middle of Northwood forest.

They were lion fodder.

She scratched around inside the sack, feeling for a seam. There had to be one, she figured, and it would be hand sewn, and quite rough.

Her fingers found what she thought might be a seam

at the bottom of the sack and she felt her way along to the end. She managed to work up a thread and pulled on it until she had a loop of cotton, which she snapped.

Starting at one end, she picked at the stitching with her fingernails until she had loosened four or five stitches, making a small hole in the bottom of the sack. Then she grabbed both sides of the seam and pulled. The seam began to open with a ripping sound.

As soon as the hole was large enough, she pulled the sack down over her head and stepped out of it, finding herself in a small clearing. It was dark in the forest at night, but the moon rose high overhead.

It painted the long grass of the clearing in long silver brushstrokes, and gave an unearthly halo to the tree canopy around them. By its light, she could make out the black shapes of her friends wrestling with their sacks on the forest floor.

"Hold still," she said to the nearest sack, and pulled quickly at the rope that was tying it shut. Avery's head popped out, her hair a mess, her eyes black with anger.

"How dare they!" she exploded. Then she stopped and looked around. "We're in the forest," she said.

"Shhh," Cecilia said, untying Evan. "There may be lions nearby."

***

It should be terrifying, Cecilia thought, *but it's somehow beautiful.* They were lost in a maze in a dark forest filled with man-eating lions, which should have been enough to have them cowering and crying on the ground. But instead Cecilia felt bold.

Perhaps she had just run out of fear. She had been using so much of it in the castle, with the King and his evil guards. Maybe fear was like water in a glass, and when you used it all up and there was nothing left in the glass, then you weren't afraid anymore.

Cecilia was not afraid.

"What do we do now?" Avery asked. "How can we get back to the castle?"

Evan was gazing up at the moon and the stars. "This way, I think."

"Do we want to return to the castle?" Cecilia asked softly.

The others turned and looked at her.

"Even if we can find our way," Cecilia said, "King Harry will just throw us in the dungeon again." She shuddered at the thought. "Maybe we should try to find our way out."

"We don't have a choice. We have to go back," Avery said. "We have to tell everybody the truth."

"It's a maze," Evan said. "We'll be lucky if we can find our way anywhere!"

"We can't stay here," Avery said. "So let's just start walking."

"We can't be too far from the castle," Evan reasoned. "It didn't take them all that long to bring us here."

"Also, they wouldn't have wanted to travel too far in the forest at night," Avery said. "Because of the lions."

"We'll go Evan's way," Cecilia said. "See where that takes us."

Where it took them was directly to the lions' den.

30
Fist Rock

THE PATH BEGAN to dip into a small ditch.

"Do you recognize this place?" Cecilia whispered.

"No, never been here before in my life," Avery whispered back, and Evan shook his head.

They had been walking for hours. Following tracks, trying to recognize paths, walking in circles for all they knew, because there was no way of identifying trees or turns in the darkness.

For half of that time they had traveled with the sound of snoring lions in their ears. They couldn't tell where the sound was coming from. In the cold dark night of the forest, the sound traveled a long way, bouncing off trees and sneaking along pathways until it could have been coming from anywhere.

The path dipped farther down into the ditch. Here, the

damp smell of the forest intensified. Snoring surrounded them. Cecilia thought it was getting louder and said so in a tiny voice.

"We can't tell where it's coming from," Avery said. "We may as well keep going for now."

They came to a bend in the path. There had been no side paths for a long time, so the only way to go was ahead.

But here there was no doubt. The snoring was much louder, and it was coming from more than one lion — more than two, probably, although it was impossible to tell for certain.

"We have to go back," Cecilia said, as quietly as she could. Her voice was barely a glimmer of sound in the still night air.

"We can't." Evan's voice was just as quiet.

"We have to," Avery said.

"We can't," Evan repeated.

"Why not?" Cecilia asked.

"Because there's a lion behind us," Evan said.

Cecilia looked back along the trail, but could see nothing. "How do you know?" she asked.

"Because I can hear it breathing," Evan said. "We must have woken it up, or maybe it couldn't sleep, or whatever. But it's been on our trail for the last ten minutes."

Cecilia listened carefully. There it was: a low rasp of breath, in and out. With all the snoring around them she hadn't noticed it before. She couldn't tell how far away it was, but it sounded close.

That was the last thing they needed. An insomniac lion.

"Why hasn't it attacked us?" she asked.

"I don't know," Evan said.

Cecilia had an idea why, but didn't want to say it out loud. She had a strong feeling that the big cat behind them might have been herding them. Pushing them toward something, or someplace.

"What do we do?" she asked.

"We have to go on," Evan said. "We can't go back."

The sloping path led them down to another small clearing, where the moonlight poured through the gap in the trees and seeped into the ground like silver blood.

At the far end of the clearing stood a huge fist-shaped rock. It was formed out of a series of flat ridges on a small cliff face that transformed into a clenched hand as they climbed into the sky.

The ridges were not flat, Cecilia realized, but covered with dark mounds of rock.

One of the mounds moved and stretched.

The mounds were lions.

Cecilia was dumbfounded. She had no idea how many lions there were roaming the forest. But just in this one place there had to be a dozen of them, sleeping on the ridges of the cliff face. She had been right. The lion behind them was herding them toward this place. The lions' den.

"What now?" Cecilia said.

"We go back," Avery said. "I'd rather face one lion than a whole pack of them."

"Pride," Evan said.

"What?" Avery's voice raised up a notch.

"A *pride* of lions, not a pack," Evan said.

"Oh, just shut up," Avery said.

A low, menacing growl came from behind them.

There was another growl, much louder now, and the snoring stopped.

"Oh no," Cecilia said.

A shape uncurled itself from the long grass in front of them. Two dots glowed. Two huge eyes. Another lion. A huge lion. They had almost walked right on top of it. Silver moonlight stained its coarse fur as it got slowly to its feet.

The other lions were rising too, forming a rough semicircle behind the large one. On the path behind her, Cecilia heard a snarl. No longer a throaty growl, this was vicious.

"We need to climb a tree," Avery said.

"They'll be on us the moment we move," Evan said.

"So stay still and become lion food," Avery said. "I'm going for a tree."

The huge lion in front of them, a male, twisted its head around and let out a roar that crashed like waves throughout the forest.

Stale meaty breath rushed along the pathway.

They could hear the footsteps of the lion behind them, closing in on them, and the big male in front took a step forward.

"It's now or never," Avery said, preparing to grab for the branches of one of the trees.

The big male tensed, ready to spring.

"Stop!" Cecilia yelled. "Stop!"

Avery stopped.

The lion stopped.

Evan stopped breathing.

"Stop!" Cecilia yelled again. Avery turned in confusion, but saw that Cecilia wasn't talking to her.

Cecilia's hand was held out in front of her as if stopping traffic, but her gesture and her voice were directed at the big lion.

The coiled tension in the big black lion's muscles

softened and it sank back a little. It turned its head one way then the other, eyeing Cecilia up and down. Then it opened its mouth and gave another roar, but much quieter this time.

"Why?" asked the lion.

31
Wise One

"BECAUSE WE'RE JUST kids," Cecilia said, trying frantically to think of a good reason why this pack of hungry lions should not eat her and her friends.

The lion considered that.

"What the heck is going on?" Avery asked.

"Just be quiet," Evan said, who clearly had some idea what was happening.

"If you are cubs," the lion said, "then you will be soft and sweet to eat."

"But not much of a meal," Cecilia said. "Don't you protect your own cubs, your babies, until they are old enough to protect themselves?"

"Of course," the old lion said. "But you are not baby lions."

"What's your name?" Cecilia asked, desperate to keep

the lion talking. If he was talking, he wasn't munching. You can't talk with your mouth full, as her mother was fond of saying.

The lion gave an answer, but there was no word in English for it. Cecilia felt that the sound was more of a title than a name. This was the leader of the pride, she was sure, but the name did not mean "leader," or "King of the lions." It felt more like "wise one," or "grandfather." A giver of advice, rather than a giver of commands.

"These are your lions," Cecilia said, meaning he was the one in charge, but his answer surprised her.

"These are my cubs," the lion said.

The other lions were all his children, he was saying. Or the children of his children.

"You are Prowler!" Cecilia realized.

This lion was one of the original two lions that had escaped from Mr. Jingle's African Safari Park over fifteen years ago. That made him very old for a lion.

"Where is Growler?" Cecilia struggled for a word that the lion would understand. "Your wife. Your female."

The lion lowered his head. "She is dead," he growled softly. "Killed by humans . . . by the small round human who lives over there." He gestured with his paw.

She knew who he was talking about. King Harry.

"What happened?" Cecilia asked.

Prowler lifted his head again and growled softly. "She came across him on one of the paths. She showed him no harm. Without warning, he shot her with a small gun. She dragged herself back home, but died the next day."

A gun! No wonder King Harry was so brave. *So much for my vision of him striding fearlessly through the forest,* Cecilia thought.

"I'm sorry about your female," she said. She was telling the truth, and she was fairly certain the lion could sense that. "The King, the small round one, is my enemy also," she said. "He cast us out into the forest so that you would eat us."

The old lion shook his whole body, starting with his head. His mane flared in the moonlight. He stared directly at her. "The small round one would like me to eat you?" He considered that. "Then we will not. Not tonight. Deer and pigs are not as plentiful as they once were in this forest, but we have all eaten today."

"Thank you," Cecilia said sincerely.

"I cannot promise for another day," the lion said. "And I cannot guarantee what other lions may do if they catch you alone in the forest. But tonight you are safe."

"Thank you," Cecilia said again. "May I touch you?"

"Touch me? Why?" the old lion asked.

"Because I want to," Cecilia said.

The lion looked at her for a moment, then nodded. Cecilia stepped forward and put her arms around the lion's neck, hugging him, feeling the coarse hair of his mane rub on her cheek and neck.

"Are you crazy?" she heard Avery say behind her.

"Thank you, Prowler," Cecilia said.

"You can let go now," Prowler said, clearly a little perturbed by all this attention in front of his pride. "And please leave now, before any of my children decide to disobey me and tear you limb from limb for a midnight snack."

Cecilia said, "But we don't know where to go. We want to get back to the castle."

The lion shook his head, clearly thinking, but not saying, how useless human beings were at simple things like finding their way around a dark forest at night. He roared at the lion behind them, the one that had been herding them.

"She will take you," Prowler said. "Be sure never to come back into this forest."

Cecilia turned around to the incredulous faces of Avery and Evan.

"What is going on?" Evan asked.

"The lions are leading us back to the castle," Cecilia said.

"Of course," Avery said, as if it was the most natural thing in the world.

***

Their guide, a young female, bounded along in front of them like an excited kitten. Cecilia did not know her name, but decided to call her Retha. Retha led them along winding path after winding path, through gorges and along ridges. They traveled in darkness, but every now and then Retha would turn back and look at them, and the glowing dots of her eyes were their guiding lights.

"You spoke to that lion," Evan said as they walked. "And he understood you."

"And he spoke back," Avery said. "And you understood him."

"And now this lion is leading us back to the castle," Evan said.

"How can that be?" Avery asked.

They were both trudging along behind her as if in a daze. They were completely bewildered by what they had seen.

"I don't really know," Cecilia said. "I've just always been able to understand what animals are saying."

"You've been talking to Rocky, too, haven't you?" Avery asked.

Cecilia nodded.

"You know what this means," Evan said slowly.

"I'm not sure," Cecilia said. "But I can't stop thinking about it ever since we saw the picture."

"It must be," Avery said. "Princess Annachanel could talk to animals and so can you. You must be a descendant of the Queen!"

"After the earthquake and the flood, the people must have settled on the lands around here. That's where you're from," Evan said.

"My family has lived in Brookfield for generations," Cecilia agreed. "On my mother's side at least."

"And if you are a descendant of Queen Annachanel, then Castle Storm and Storm Gorge are rightfully yours," Evan said.

"What about your mother?" Avery said. "Wouldn't that make her the Queen?"

"My mother died having me," Cecilia said. "So I guess it would be me. But talking to animals is no proof that I am related to Annachanel."

"It is to me," Evan said.

There was a low growl from in front of them. Retha stiffened, her hairs raised, ready to attack. She hissed like a cat.

And suddenly Rocky was there, bounding down the path toward them. Barking wildly, he threw himself at Retha, trying to defend Cecilia, Avery, and Evan from the lion.

"No!" Cecilia shouted, but it was too late.

The Samoyed hurled himself at the lion, who batted him aside with one powerful paw as though she was swatting a fly. Rocky jumped back to his feet and leaped back into the attack, despite Cecilia screaming at both of them to stop.

A huge backhand swipe from Retha lifted Rocky clean off his feet, smashing him into the trunk of a tarblood tree.

There was a crack, and Rocky toppled back to the ground and lay still.

32
An Announcement

AVERY CARRIED ROCKY back to the castle.

Cecilia wanted to, but although Rocky was thin, he was too heavy for her. Even Avery struggled with the weight.

Rocky was still breathing, but his breath was shallow, and when Cecilia put her ear to his chest, his heartbeat was faint.

He did not move, and although she was no veterinarian, Cecilia felt in her heart that Rocky did not have long in this world.

Retha led them the rest of the way back to the castle, but remained in the shadows of the path as they walked through the clearing up to the cliff face.

The morning light was in the sky, although the sun had not yet risen. Already the tarblood trees were starting to give off their foggy mist. The trunks shimmered as the water evaporated and rose, forming the dense fog that would soon envelop the forest.

The door in the base of the cliff was open just a crack, but widened quickly as they walked into the clearing.

Mrs. Proctor's worried face looked out. "Evan! Avery! Cecilia!" She saw the shape in Avery's arms. "Rocky!"

She seemed flustered. "Where have you . . . ? What happened to . . . ? Why . . . ?"

"Where's the King?" Cecilia asked with narrowed eyes, ignoring all the questions.

"The King? He . . . we were all so worried," Mrs. Proctor said. "Why did you run off like that? I . . . Rocky was sniffing and scratching at the door. When I opened it, he just took off. Oh, what have I done?"

By the time they reached the main courtyard it was full of people. Mrs. Proctor was carrying Rocky now, her face full of tears. Whether the tears were for Rocky or for the safe return of Cecilia and the twins, Cecilia couldn't tell.

The royal quarters were at the very top of the castle, so the King and his goons were probably the last to hear the commotion. They were the only people not there. Everybody else crowded around the three of them, demanding answers.

Evan and Avery's parents had each grabbed one of the

twins, and were hanging on to them as if they would never let them go again.

"They told us that you had escaped, that Avery and Evan were your accomplices, and that the three of you had run off into the forest," Mrs. Proctor said.

Cecilia was exhausted. They had been walking through the forest maze all night — most of it in circles — and the constant fear had used up a lot of energy. Plus, she was dreadfully worried about Rocky.

Suddenly she found herself curiously energetic. Somehow the excitement and anger were overriding everything else.

"We escaped, all right," she said, noticing Tony Baloney at the back of the crowd. *How will we explain all this to him?* she wondered.

"But we didn't run off into the forest," she continued. "We were going to hide out in the gorge, but we were kidnapped, tied up in sacks, and left in the middle of Northwood."

The crowd gasped.

"At night!" Mrs. Proctor asked. "Didn't you run into any lions?"

"Yes, lots," Avery said, but Cecilia gave her a quick glance, and she didn't elaborate further.

"Is that what happened to Rocky?" Mrs. Proctor asked.

"Yes," Cecilia said, "Rocky thought a lion was attacking us, so he tried to save us. He's a hero."

Someone found a blanket and Mrs. Proctor laid Rocky down on it in the middle of the courtyard.

Here in the light Cecilia could see the long gashes that ran across Rocky's chest and down onto his belly. His eyes were shut and his breathing seemed to be fading away slowly to nothing.

"Who did this to you?" Mrs. Proctor started to ask, but it was clear from her face that she knew the answer before she even finished asking the question.

And so did everybody else in the courtyard.

At that moment King Harry burst down the stairs from the royal quarters. He wore a silk dressing gown, but it was flapping open to reveal a white T-shirt and tacky Mickey Mouse boxer shorts. Grizzly, Weasel, Wolf, and Skunk trailed closely behind.

"The thief has returned," the King cried. "A traitor, a spy, and an escaped prisoner to boot."

An angry murmur ran through the crowd.

"Seize them!" the King shouted. The four guards moved forward, only to find their way blocked by a swell of people.

Cecilia looked around at Avery and Evan, who both nodded.

"You tell them," Avery said.

A pair of strong hands lifted her up onto a stone table.

She glanced at Rocky one more time before starting to speak.

"What King Harry doesn't want you to know," she said in a strong, clear voice, "is that there is a picture in the royal quarters, in the drawing room, of Baron Mendoza."

An angry murmur went through the crowd at the very mention of that name.

"If you see the picture," Cecilia said, "I am sure that you will agree that King Harry of Storm is really Harry Mendoza, a descendant of the Baron himself. And what's more . . . "

Up to that stage it had been just a theory, based on the picture, but the King's reaction provided the proof. An enraged King Harry screamed at his guards.

With big Sergeant Lee leading the charge, they formed a flying wedge and hurtled into the crowd, knocking people out of their way as they headed for Cecilia.

She squealed with fright, but could do nothing as the huge shape of Sergeant Lee pushed the last person out of the way and stood right in front of her. He reached out to grab her — to hurt her. His hands were just closing on her arms, when there was a solid dull thudding noise, and Sergeant Lee went flying sideways. He collided with the wall and sprawled across the ground, looking up in a daze at the people around him.

"Boomphah!" said Tony Baloney.

The other guards tried to attack Tony, but there were suddenly hands everywhere, grabbing them, pinning their arms back. That just left Tony and Sergeant Lee alone in an empty circle of space.

"You stupid, brainless moron," Sergeant Lee yelled, groggily getting back to his feet. "You village idiot, you feeble-minded tar man." He moved toward Tony, his hands clenching up into fists, but there was something in Tony's eyes. Cecilia saw it, and Lee must have seen it too. The ice-cold fury that stabbed out of Tony's eyes would have frightened any creature. *No wonder the black lions keep away from him,* Cecilia thought.

The sergeant began to back away. The other guards struggled, but were ensnared in the arms of the crowd, like flies in a spider's web.

Tony advanced. Sergeant Lee backed away, terrified, his hands up in front of him as if trying to push Tony away.

He's just a bully, Cecilia thought. *And, like most bullies,*

he's really a big coward. Sergeant Lee tripped and fell backward, sitting on his behind as Tony loomed over him.

Suddenly, there was a crashing, booming explosion of a sound, and chips of stone fell from the ceiling of the entryway. Everybody froze, and all eyes turned to the King, who had produced a small black pistol from somewhere in his robe and was waving it in all directions.

Sergeant Lee took advantage of the shock to jump back to his feet and run toward the King. The other guards wriggled out of the clutches of the crowd and retreated toward the stairs. They backed away slowly as the King waved the gun around.

There was a surging roar from the crowd, and the King turned and fled. His pudgy, hairy legs in their stupid cartoon boxer shorts pumped up and down like pistons as he fled up the stairs, with the guards close behind him.

Then nothing remained but a stunned silence, and they heard the big wooden doors at the entrance to the royal quarters slam shut.

Evan had climbed up onto the table and was trying to get everybody's attention. Avery put two fingers in her mouth and whistled. The piercing sound cut through the crowd like a sword.

"Ladies and gentlemen," Evan announced, in a very

formal-sounding voice. "There was another picture in the drawing room, revealing even more startling information."

He paused, then held out a hand toward Cecilia. "I would like all of you to meet the great-great-granddaughter of Queen Annachanel, the great-great-great-granddaughter of King Danyon and Queen Natassia, and the rightful owner of Castle Storm and all its Environs — Her Royal Highness, Queen Cecilia of Storm."

There was dead silence in the room.

Then a remarkable thing happened. Big Tony, who was totally deaf and could not have heard a word of what Evan had said, turned to face Cecilia, dropped to one knee, and bowed his head.

That started it.

Every person in the room turned toward Cecilia and, all at once, dropped to one knee and bowed their heads. Bowing to their new Queen.

"Oh my word," said Cecilia, which was beginning to become a habit.

33
SOLVING THE MYSTERY

QUEEN CECILIA CALLED a meeting in the throne room. The first and last one she would ever hold. It was only at the insistence of everyone else that she finally stepped up toward the big stone throne and sat on it.

Rocky sat at her side, and her hand toyed with his long white fur as she waited for everybody to come in and be seated.

On her other side, resplendent in the bright-blue tunic of the royal guards, sat Tony Baloney. Every time that Cecilia said she didn't think she needed a royal guard, he just pointed to his ear and shook his head.

Avery and Evan sat at the head of the long table. They were now officially her royal advisors.

That was what Evan said they were, anyway. He said it was an important position and that he and Avery were quite serendipitous to have been chosen. Cecilia couldn't bring herself to tell him it was the wrong word again.

It had been three days since Harry disappeared. He and his goons had spent several days barricaded inside the royal chambers. Then one morning the door had been wide open and all of them were gone.

That same day, Rocky had opened his eyes for the first time and looked around him, and Cecilia had cried and hugged him. He licked her, and she asked him to stop because it was all gooey. He said he was sorry, but he couldn't help it.

He was a dog, after all.

The royal crown had vanished with Harry, but to be honest, it was probably too big and heavy for a ten-year-old girl anyway. Instead, Cecilia wore the beautiful, and now spotlessly clean, golden tiara they had found in the nursery.

Cecilia surveyed the room, almost exploding with the news she had to give everyone.

The room was full of smiles.

"People of Storm," Cecilia said in her biggest voice. What her teacher, Mr. Treegarden, would have called her "outside voice." She continued, "I am not sure that I am ready to be your Queen." There was a murmur of disagreement but she spoke on, and the voices fell silent.

"And I am not going to be your Queen."

The murmur was back, a little concerned now.

"Not because I do not wish to be, but because I have some good news for you."

Dead silence. A hush of anticipation.

"Today, we are leaving Castle Storm," Cecilia announced.

It took ten minutes for the noise to subside so she could explain further.

"The answer was always right under my nose, but I was too stupid to see it," she said. "Until Harry and his goons escaped. We'd thought that Harry knew a secret path out through the forest maze, but after they left, the front door of the castle was still bolted. So I realized that their passage to the outside world must be from within the castle itself."

She stopped for a moment, enjoying the anticipation on all their faces.

"And then I thought that there must be an entrance to another secret passage in the royal quarters, so we searched there. But all we found were empty beer bottles and old pizza boxes. While I was wandering around the castle, searching, a little blue bird flew in and perched on the windowsill."

There were some curious looks and some nodding

heads. Everybody knew the speedy little blue birds that darted around the castle.

"And that's when I finally realized what had been under my nose all along. Come with me."

She stood and walked from the throne room, forcing herself not to run, a perplexed crowd following in her wake.

She led them outside to the courtyard, where a large rock had been placed near the beginning of the water channel that fed the waterfall and the birdbath.

With a nod from Cecilia, big Tony put both hands around the rock and heaved, lowering it into the channel and blocking the water.

In a second or two the stream across the courtyard was almost dry, and the waterfall slowed to a mere trickle.

Cecilia led the way down to the lower level and pointed to the waterfall. The velvet curtain of water was drawn back, revealing a dark window into unknown places.

"The birdbath was the clue," Cecilia said. "This is the start of the passage. This is how Harry brought in his supplies, and how he escaped. I even know where the tunnel will take us."

She looked around excitedly, overjoyed for a whole bunch of reasons. She was overjoyed that she was about to see her parents and Jana again, that she would be able to eat normal food, that she would be back in the real world.

"Where does it come out?" Mrs. Proctor asked.

Cecilia reached out and grasped the little golden bird statue.

"The Church of the Yellow Bird."

34
What It Was All About

IT WAS ALL about truffles. That was one thing Cecilia hadn't figured out, mainly because she didn't know anything about truffles.

Truffles are very rare, and because of that they are a very expensive delicacy used in fine French cooking.

White truffles are the most prized and the most rare, and because of that they are the most expensive.

A single pound of white truffles can be worth thousands of dollars.

It so happened that the beech forest along the riverbank in Storm Gorge was one of the best places in the world to find truffles.

"King" Harry was harvesting them, sneaking them through the waterfall in the middle of the night, shipping them out through the underground tunnel on wooden carts, and selling them at a huge profit, which he and the guards were sharing.

Cecilia and the others figured that out when they found the carts and empty truffle sacks deep underground in the secret passage.

She was wrong about the Church of the Yellow Bird, but only slightly. The church had been built next to a ruined monastery, which was much, much older.

It was from the cellar of the ruined Yellow Bird monastery that Cecilia and the others emerged on a bright sunny morning, shielding their eyes and marveling at the blue dome of the sky, which they had not seen for many years — or in Avery and Evan's case, ever!

It was a Friday and nobody was at church that day, but a whole crowd of people appearing suddenly on an island in the middle of a lake was not going to go unnoticed. Before long, there was a small fleet of boats, canoes, and pedal boats ferrying the newcomers across the lake to the shore.

Cecilia, as befits a queen, was last to leave the island, finally departing in the back of a small dinghy rowed by the pastor of the church himself.

Rocky, of course, was by her side, although he was weak and just lay with his head on her lap the whole way.

The pastor told her that her parents were on their way back from the city where they had been trying to organize a large search party.

So when Cecilia stepped off the boat and onto the small dock on the shore of the lake, it was not her mother or father who was there to greet her, but a huge fluffy pillow of a woman who threw her arms around her so energetically that the two of them almost toppled off the dock into the water.

"Bam, bam, bam!" Jana shouted. There were tears in Jana's eyes and snot running out of her nose. "Bam, bam, bam. Oh, this is a beautiful day. The sun has shone down on Jana today and brought my little child back."

Cecilia tried to talk, but there was no getting a word in against Jana.

"Oh, hallelujah and praise the Lord, child, I thought you were eaten by them lions."

"I almost was." Cecilia gasped for breath, submerged in Jana's flowery blouse. "Come on, you have to meet Avery and Evan."

And Jana's love overflowed some more.

In fact, that day it was a true deluge.

35
The End of the Story

AND THAT'S THE end of the story. The strange (and probably not true) story of Cecilia Undergarment and the black lions of Northwood.

The castle became a tourist attraction. Some of the people who had lived there even returned to work as tour guides or actors in "reenactment scenes." The difference was that now they could leave whenever they wanted.

Queen Cecilia visited regularly, just to keep an eye on things, and to watch out for her royal subjects. For the lions, nothing changed. Although every once in a while Prowler would stroll down to the clearing, and Queen Cecilia would go out to meet him, and they would chat for a while about the weather and the goings-on in the forest.

Or did they? It depends on whether what I am telling you is true, or just a big fat farty fib.

But remember, not everything is entirely what it seems. Nor is it otherwise.

THE END